I0584200

The Arch of Fire

The Arch of Fire (Banhi Balaya) received
Odisha Sahitya Academy Award in 1989

The Arch of Fire

The Arch of Fire (Banhi Balaya) received
Odisha Sahitya Academy Award in 1989

Prof. Madan Mohan Mishra

Translated by
Dr Tapan K Panda

BLACK EAGLE BOOKS
2021

BLACK EAGLE BOOKS

USA address:
7464 Wisdom Lane
Dublin, OH 43016

India address:
E/312, Trident Galaxy, Kalinga Nagar,
Bhubaneswar-751003, Odisha, India

E-mail: info@blackeaglebooks.org
Website: www.blackeaglebooks.org

First International Edition Published by
BLACK EAGLE BOOKS, 2021

THE ARCH OF FIRE
by **Prof. Madan Mohan Mishra**
Translated by **Dr Tapan K Panda**

Cover & Interior Design: Ezy's Publication

ISBN- 978-1-64560-183-8 (Paperback)
Library of Congress Control Number: 2021937184

Printed in United States of America

Foreword

It's overwhelming to write a few lines for my beloved father and his award winning novel, "Banhi Balay." Literally I have no words to write for him or about him. Not a single day has passed in my life when I didn't remember him. Needless to say, he was and has been my greatest inspiration. I don't count the number of books he has penned down; I always fondly remember how he lived his life like a true poet. He was a poet by birth. He could utter poems effortlessly but forget them the next moment. Neither he, nor we, his off springs, had the thought of noting them down. He would say innumerable lines spontaneously which had a deep poetic sense and all of us would recite those for some days until a new poem came up and this used to go on. He and we have lost them all, for ever. He was never very careful about his stories or poems and lost more than what he kept. His love for books, hymns, languages, food, teaching and last but not the least, for life, was unbelievable.

When he was only ten months old, his father renounced his family life for the quest of truth and became a Sannyasi(monk). He was not so fortunate to have his father's company, blessings or love but his dedication to see his father, at least once, made him a traveller in his youth. He had been to all the corners of this vast country in search of his father and was finally successful. He met him once, for a very short time, though the monk was reluctant to recognise him. Life denied him paternal love and attention from an early age, but what an amazing father he himself was!

He was the first and only son in the family after seven generations, so he had no brothers, as such. But that didn't devoid us of an extended family's love and attention. In fact we don't even remember how many younger brothers he had who were very loyal to him. He knew the art of creating and maintaining relationships. His face had a tremendously soft look and his heart was like that of a small child with a great sense of humour. I clearly remember the evening, the meeting in the Suchana Bhawan where he was awarded for this very novel. I was in the audience. As soon as he was free, he bought me a pair of bangles from the then small Lalchand Jewellery Store in Master Canteen with the prize money. I had never asked him, for sure, so was amazed to get such a gift, at a young age. I still have those bangles around my wrist, which are his blessings on me.

He never commanded or dictated us to read or write. We were all brought up seeing our father reading and writing. Books were his prized possession; he never thought of buying land or any household gadget. Books were something which used to reach our home through post at regular intervals. From Encyclopaedia Britannica to Ramayana, from Readers' Digest to the famous Bengali magazine Desh, from Sarat Chandra to Surendra Mohanty, he had them all in his big almirah. I can't remember a single occasion when my father would get delighted or disheartened because of our annual results. But he would become instantly happy when he found anyone of us picking up a book from his collection or reading one. A book is a book, maybe of any genre, he never ever said us what to read. A book was always with him, while traveling, while attending anyone of us during our sickness, even till late nights.

He had a vast range of knowledge, from Sanskrit to medicine, from cricket to food; he had an answer for all my queries. He was an amazing orator and so, was often invited to address gatherings. He was modern and liberal, yet had a great sense of respect for our traditions. We had more faith in him than in any doctor. During our childhood, whenever we fell sick, we waited for him to chant the Sree Bagalamukhi stotram for our recovery. He was a magician for us.

But as children, we have not inherited even a small portion of his brilliant attitude. Always very smartly dressed, my father had a heart full of love. It's very unfortunate that when we are finally getting time to realise his sacrifices and deeds, he is not with us. I am no one to introduce or estimate his literary work. It's a great pleasure to see his book being translated into English, a language which he mastered and spoke so eloquently.

I can go on and on for unlimited pages about my father. I am very thankful to my dear friend Tapan who has loved reading this novel and translated the same for a wider audience. I was also elated to read the note from Sanket, My nephew and the third generation writer from the family for his note on my father and his beloved grandfather.

Hope this book finds a larger audience now and more people get to connect with my father.

Dr. Hiranmayee Mishra
Author of Gotie Barsaa Raati Ra Kahani,
Megha Pakshi Ra Gita and Kalijai & Other Stories

From Grandson to his Grand Father

The first memory of Prof. Madan Mohan Mishra, Bapa to me, that I have is him sitting on a wobbly chair in the courtyard of our ancestral home in Achyutrajpur. He is gleaming in the halos of the sesame and coconut oil he has applied over his body. My sister and I are sitting at the foot of the chair with anticipation in our eyes. He is making a paan (Betel leaf) from his DIY paan-box, and we know once done a story, we are waiting with bated breath, will arrive. We do not want to interrupt his creative process, so there is a silence all around us. He clears his throats, pushes the betel to a corner of his cheeks and begins. "Do you know the story of …"

As it happens with generations, much of his life exists only as feeble memories in my mind. He was born to teach. If it was not in colleges, it was in our houses, at our temples and on our bed. Whether it was a snippet from the Ramayana, an excellent card game, the taste of a particular species of fish or some obscure quote from Che Guevarra, you were never too far from learning something from him.

"Banhi Balaya" (The Arch of Fire) was first published around the time I was born. India was on the cusp of liberalisation in an economic and social context. There were signs of significant progress, and prosperity which was well reflected in the upper echelons of society. However, in what has been the biggest failure of the Indian political and corporate class, the progress had only trickled down in minimal amounts to the poorest sections of the society. A society which already had a host of crippling injustices to deal with in Casteism, Woman and Child Welfare and Poverty, now had to face all the same injustices multiplied manifold.

Social democracy suddenly did not seem to be the great panacea that the makers of India had promised it would be. The spark that began in Naxalbari, West Bengal in 1967 was now raging across the poorest states of India, Odisha, Andhra Pradesh and Bihar. As one of the characters, Chinmaya Chakrabarty puts it "We don't want minor changes and enculturation, we want a radical upheaval". It is into this social context; Prof. Mishra puts his protagonist Shrikumar and all his other characters. As the story advances, the characters are all wrapped up in conflicts which are believable and intensely captivating. But that is not all, Prof. Mishra, through his characters, challenges the reader's beliefs too. Therein lays the essence of Banhi Balaya.

Our worlds have become a vast, towering stage. In an era of short attention spans, more and more people are joining in this race to gain attention. So where does that leave a novel written more than 30 years ago? Why does that need to be translated? Yes, it won prestigious awards and much praise from contemporary writers, but why do more people need to read it now? The answer lies sadly in the societies that we currently live in. We are more divided as a country than we have ever been. The unprivileged still fight the same battles that they fought 30, 40 or 70 years ago. Rapes, killings, the lynching of the powerless have become norms. What is of utmost importance is that the privileged castes examine the power they hold over our societies.

We need to know that our society is aligned in a way where we are given a get out of jail card for every digression we commit. And in that this timeless novel can help you start. For example, there is a passage in the novel where the radical Chinmaya Chakrabarty compares the various government schemes for the Scheduled Caste and Tribes as the broken bits of biscuits you give to your dog. That compelling part is one among many such passages whose motivation is not to turn you to a revolutionary but to understand where the anger is coming from. Only in understanding that and making reversals for that can we salvage the age-old idea of India.

It has been nearly six years since Prof. Mishra died leaving behind unfinished stories, unwritten novels. For his family and friends, he left behind a whole treasure trove of memories. Of his jovial nature, of his love for fish, of his many stories. But memories are susceptible to the invincible powers of the time. It gets ravaged and uprooted unless you hide them in the nooks and crannies that a book provides. You tie emotions with black words. And invoke them when you need them the most. I hope this book keeps your memories as timeless as it did mine.

Sanket Mishra
Singapore

PREFACE

'The Arch of Fire' is based on the Naxalite' tactice against the Indian State. Seizing land from oppressors and redistributing it amongst the peasants has been the aim of the Naxalites since its creation. In 1967, oppressed peasants inspired by the communist movement raised their bows and arrows against the feudal landowners in Naxalbari. Naxalites, raised their upgraded, more sophisticated weapons against mining corporations and development projects which threatened to expel indigenous tribes or Adivasis from their ancestral lands in order to exploit the mineral-rich soil. The Naxalite movement as we know it today, its emergence is a result of the various fragmentations of communist ideologies in India over time. Hence, in order to comprehend the nature of Naxalism, one must first delve into its own tumultuous history.

We have read many novels and stories on similar plots in the majority of Indian languages. What makes this novel so unique? Why is this a classic written in Odia literature? These are the intriguing questions that I searched for when I read this novel for the first time. I had intended at that time to translate this novel for English audience. I read the novel as a reader only. I was influenced by the Naxalite movement and quite impacted by the stories, poems written on the same theme. In fact, my first short story collection is also titled as 'Naxalite and Other Stories". The first story on my book is about the common man's struggle and police atrocities (The Naxalite) while the second story was more metaphorical based on inequity and the philosophy of identity (The Stupid Man and the Cap). So I was biased by the domain of naxalism and the idea of an equitable society when I got this novel from Hiranmayee for my reading.

As I moved ahead on the storyline, I could see the fine craft of bringing soft romance brewing between the protagonists. This was subtle by approach yet very evident and was quite soothing for the idealism and righteous track of equity and justice. The mind didn't have to really struggle with the thought of 'catching fire by the tail' and running around in search of water to extinguish the fire. The parallel tracks followed either through dialogues or through descriptions by the novelist only brought a gentle smile to the reader. The common thought that flows in this amazing design of crafting the story makes one feel 'aha, this is also possible!'.

The novel is on humanity and universality of love. The sketches and scenes from the most beautiful district of Koraput have been able to capture the virgin landscape of Odisha. The author brings in his maturity in the idea of 'pitching'- it is more situational driven than character driven. Many times, he is like a painter- who does the sketch, context and silhouette before bringing the characters- so the flow is more visual than textual. I have seen these kinds of expressions in a few Indian authors. This also shows the maturity of the writer as he has written this novel at quite an advanced stage of his life.

I re-read this novel a few times, when I decided to translate it into English. Honestly speaking, I had not read him before (compared to his daughter's writings). So I had to take some time to look at his unique craft, subtle flow of romance in the most uncommon landscape of naxalism and trust his words.

Translation is a difficult proposition particularly when you handle a novel which has more country words (deshaja sabda). I have tried to make an approximation. I had to make a choice between – making my translation being honest and true to the words and making them beautiful. If I am honest with words and flow, I will lose the opportunity to reflect on the grandeur of design in the novel and if I make it beautiful then it will not be an actual 'translation'. I have taken a mid-path with a bias towards beauty. My reliance on structure and grammar is lesser here than what I intend to communicate. I hope the reader will bear with me for these fallacies. Tapasya Foundation has a mission to make some of the classic novels and short story collections be preserved and made available for English audiences and particularly for the new generation of readers who unfortunately cant/don't read Odia literature. This translation is a part of realizing this vision of the foundation. I wish to thank the family of Prof Madan Mohan Mishra for permitting me to try my hands with translation of this novel.

I never met Prof Madan Mohan Mishra in my lifetime but I am sure if I would have met him in the past, I would have talked about this novel with him for hours on his curiosity and creativity to experiment such a theme. I owe all the flaws in this translation as English as a language is very miser in its word inventory to have parallel expressions for many natural Odia words. This work was done during Corona time last year when I returned home from Mumbai. My wife (Julie) advised me one day to pursue creative exercise which I had always neglected due to my focus on academic writing and research on management. I have realized the only way to return back to the fold of creative pursuit is through contribution only – doesn't matter the depth and width of the same. I read a few sections to my Son Tejas and tried to take his views (he is a non-Odia reading English fiction and non-fiction reader who studied technical and creative writing as part of his Bachelor program) and that helped me quite a lot in the trans-creation process.

I wish to thank Mr Satya Patnaik of Black Eagle Books, USA who is equally passionate about taking Odia literature to global audience. This book including few of my other translations is an attempt by Tapasya Foundation in partnership with Black Eagle Books to take Odia classics to non-Odia reading audience, particularly the new generation who never read Odia literature due to their inability to read Odia. The books that I have translated including The Infidel, Autobiography of a Queen, Five Ways to Kill Rama, Nata and Jambuloka are an attempt to connect the millennial with Odia literature. A book is as good as its cover- that's a saying. I wish to thank Mr Ashok Parida to not only design this book but painstakingly read the novel to conceptualize the cover with his visual metaphors. I also thank the family of Late Prof Madan Mohan Mishra for allowing me to translate this masterpiece.

I will be happy if you buy this book and give it to your non-Odia reading child. Who knows- with writings like this - they may return back and start reading literature written in our mother tongue. This will make us at Tapasya Foundation realize our vision of reconnecting Millennial with their roots.

Happy Reading!

Dr Tapan K Panda
Hyderabad
tapanpanda@gmail.com

Chapter-1

Shrikumar got down from the train, holding his khadi handbag.

It was a small station near Andhra and Odisha border. Passenger trains stop at this station. During morning and evening, many people weren't seen in the station. Other than a few small businessmen returning from Ichhapuram or Palasha, beetle shop owners, and a few hawkers no one gets down in this station. In the station, there was the Assistant Station Master's office .At the backside, there was an open waiting room. At a distance there were two to three asbestos thatched railways quarter constructed for the railway employees. In total, 6-7 railway employees stay here. At the back side of the waiting room there was a stretch of a vast forest.

It was evening and the Station Master's room was lighted with a lamp. The train left- maybe he will finish a few of his work and leave for the day. Shrikumar slowly walked towards the Station Master's office.

"Can you please tell me; how far is Govindpur from here"? The mother tongue of the Station Master was Telugu but he could speak in Odia. He answered in English- Very far, almost 3 miles away, inside the forest, how will you go there in the night?-there is also the fear of wild animals in the darkness of the forest.

Shrikumar looked towards the backside of the station. How will he go? Shankar told that either he will come or send someone. But, he couldn't see anyone in the platform. He has come after receiving the message from him so it's necessary for him to go. He took out the small torch from his bag. He had loaded it with batteries while coming from Koraput. He thought that will be enough for him.

He asked- Is there anyone who is going to Govindpur from here? I can go with someone or at least, kindly let me know the way.

The Station Master was looking at him with suspicious eyes. He looked at him once and then looked at the open waiting room. Six soldiers were sitting there with their guns and a person who may be an officer was rolling tobacco to make a cigarette. They weren't in the uniform or the cap. Their duty was to protect this small station from the destruction caused by the Naxalite movement in Andhra and Odisha border. The station Master asked- Do you have any important work? Is it necessary to go at night? Otherwise, stay here and go in the early morning. Of course, there is no such facility to stay here. It was clear that he was in a confused state of mind in the way he spoke. Shrikumar said-I have to meet a friend. He is very sick and is bedridden. Maybe if I go in the morning..... He didn't speak much and tried to make him understand through his gestures that if he doesn't go in the night, then there will be a problem. "He had sent a message that he will send someone, maybe he couldn't because of some problem". The Station Master raised his hand and said; among the bushes in the forest there is a narrow trail. Take that narrows path and go. After two miles take a turn to the right. Ok Goodbye! The Station Master went into his office.

Shrikumar took his bag, crossed the waiting room, and came to the road. He looked at his wrist watch- It was fifteen minutes to seven. When he was walking, two of the soldiers were indifferently looking at him. He looked down and start walking on the trail.

Why didn't Shankar come? He had sent a message to come by the 23rd evening train and to get down in the station. What can be the reason for not coming after sending the message for so many times? Did the police raid in between? If they would have left Govindpur, then where will he go in this deep forest? How will he come to know about Prasanta? The road seemed elevated and difficult to walk.

Suddenly he stopped, thought something, and opened his bag. He took out the stethoscope from his bag and hung it around his neck. The stethoscope looked brighter in comparison to his khadi shirt, khadi dhoti, and dusty sandals. He walked ahead carefully.

After walking for a few feet, he was startled, he stood there. He saw two men standing on the road. From where and how did they come he couldn't make out. They were dressed like the farmers of Andhra Pradesh. Both of them were wearing the dhoti in a criss-cross way. One of them had a bundle of wood on his head and an axe on his shoulder. He was wearing a half sleeve vest. Both of them had beards on their face. It seemed as if they were waiting for someone. Shrikumar walked towards them. Both the men looked at him but didn't speak anything. Shrikumar asked them-How far is Govindpur from here?

One of them looked at him with his sharp eyes, and asked- Is your name Dr. Shrikumar Das? Did you come from Koraput? Shrikumar nodded his head in approval. The man said briefly- Let's go! Shrikumar asked- Did

Shankar send you? The man said-Yes, he had told us to come.

Both of them started walking on that narrow path. The road was uneven. There were ups and downs in the road. On both sides there was dense forest. With the help of the torch light Shrikumar was walking cautiously. Sometimes he stumbled. One of them was walking in front of him and the man with a bundle of wood on his head was walking behind him. The man who was walking in front of him was strong and stout, fair and was almost 35 to 40 years old. He was a little bald from the front side. He couldn't notice the man walking behind him properly, but he was a little thin and dark.

Shrikumar asked -How is the health of Prasanta? The man walking in the front replied- You can go and have a look .Shrikumar again asked-Wasn't Shankar supposed to come'? The reply was- He isn't there. The man who was behind him said- He had been to the guest house. Shrikumar felt that the answer was a little inept. He asked-Guest house? Is there a guest house in this forest? The man walking in the front said-No, no he is cracking a joke. Yesterday the police called him as they suspected him.Leave it! Is there any necessity to discuss it on the way? We don't like to discuss this in open space.

Open space! Shrikumar was astonished. It was almost between 7pm to 8 pm, but it was lone like midnight. Who will listen to what they are talking in this utter darkness?

The man walking ahead suddenly stopped .He said- Dr.Das, you may find a little difficulty here. Look! Whether you can walk or not'?

Shrikumar focused his torchlight in the forward direction. One of the rivers from the mountain had made its way through the mountain and has run through the plains. There was a deep gorge. The river was almost 20 to 22 feet wide. On it was two pieces of bamboos. The bamboos were tied in between by the wild twining vines (Laee).But how will he cross the river walking on these bamboos? He showed the torchlight. In the meantime, his co-traveler with the wood bundle on his head crossed it without any difficulty. Shrikumar very cautiously kept his feet. He started shivering in fear. The other co-traveler held him from the back. He said-Hold my hand and walk. Shrikumar asked-Aren't you afraid? While walking he answered-Fear? Yes, in the beginning, I was afraid, but now this river is like our protection shield. Otherwise, who knows we would have been there or not. Shrikumar held his hand and went to the other side. His co- traveler from the other side slowly pulled the two bamboos and threw them in the forest. He said- Doctor, it's not so easy to cross the river and come to this side. During the rainy season this small river is wild and furious. That's why this side of the river is still safe.

Shrikumar was surprised! These people stay in the forest and have sharp eyes and know about each minute detail. The man with the wooden bundle on his head was still standing.

Shrikumar looked at the surrounding. Now the road was steeply down and a little bit of carelessness can make one fall. In between, he had stumbled a few times and had injured his leg in two or three places. The moon was shining brightly. At a distance in the patches of darkness, he could see an open space. There was a hut with a thatched roof in which there was a room like a hall. The house was surrounded by thorny bushes and varieties of creepers so that one can't make out whether there is a house or not unless noticed from nearby. The man who was walking ahead went and knocked on the door twice or thrice. The door opened. Shrikumar went inside the house. A small Petromax light was burning in the room, but on both sides, it was covered with a dark cover in such a way that no one can trace the light from outside.

There was a rope bed near the door. Shrikumar went and sat on that bed. The door was closed.

Chapter-2

Shrikumar was very tired and he laid down on that bed. His kurta and vest were drenched in sweat. After 10-15 minutes he felt a little better. He got up and took out his wet kurta (shirt) and vest and looked around to put it for drying. There was a stick attached to the wall. He hanged the wet kurta and vests on it and took out a bed sheet from his bag, covered his body and sat on the bed, and looked around the house carefully.

In the room, there were few mats woven in date leaves were scattered. The area of the house was almost 25 feet by 15 feet. There were eight of them in the house, including my co-traveler. In one of the corners of the house was kept a packing box and a suitcase. on the other corner there was a table and on its books, notebooks and papers were piled up. A poster was stuck on the wall which was on the backside of the table on which the pictures of Marx, Lenin, and Mao Tse Tung were pasted and below that in red was written something in Bengali which means – Mass revolution or the rebel is never defeated .He takes rest to get prepared and fight back in the battle again.

Shrikumar was surprised as there was a ghostly silence in the house. All were silent- to ask a question- or to discuss among themselves- which is the greatest gift of nature to mankind wasn't necessary for them. There was nothing to discuss among them-their devotion towards work and the difficulties that they faced had made them silent. Leaving aside my co-travellers, there were five men and three women. They were all aged between 20 to 25 years.

A young man was busy painting something with a paintbrush and colours. In between, he was measuring with a small scale. Near him, two of them were bending and looking at his drawing style. It may be a map, which he was drawing. On the map, the river, railroad, and the mountain were marked. A young lady was busy noting down something from a book in a small notebook. Another young lady was busy mending the clothes with thread and needle.

In the mean time, one of my co-traveller was busy lighting a stove and a young lady was helping him. After the stove was lighted a small vessel filled with water was kept on it. Slowly the water started boiling. Then he asked-Doctor, would you like to have some tea first or would you like to check the patient and then have tea?

Shrikumar was noticing all these activities half listlessely.As soon as he heard the word 'Patient' he woke up from his slumbers and sat down. He said-I have come so far to see the patient. But he is in Govindpur. The co-traveler said- where is the facility for us to stay in Govindpur? Where would you have come if Govindpur name wouldn't have been mentioned? This area doesn't have a specific name in the forest and if any name would have been there, then it would have been difficult to mention.

When the water kept on the stove started boiling, condensed milk and tea powder was added to it. The tea was ready in a few minutes. Shrikumar was badly in need of tea. He took two to three sips of tea. He said- Now is it not necessary for us to know and introduce each other?

His co-traveler said- Look! Doctor, we have left behind

the age-old courtesy, and the ethos For you, name and identity is a matter of anxiousness- nothing more than that. But for us, name and identity mean a lot- maybe lifelong imprisonment or a death sentence.

Shrikumar became a little conscious. Maybe what he said is true- death warrant is hanging on the head of each person present over here, therefore an unknown person like him, who is far away from their philosophy of life, not to reveal their identity in front of him is quite natural.

Still, with a little bit of agitation, he said-It's a little bit difficult to interact without knowing each other. Human beings aren't like cattle. That's why a name is given to them and they are called by that name- to reveal the identity of oneself depends on the faith.

It's quite normal for you, doctor, to misunderstand us. But, we are far away from trivial things like misunderstanding, false prestige, and pride- that too willingly. You are talking about trust- the police have so many ways to extract the secrets from you even though you don't want to reveal it. Have you heard about the word 'Third degree'? That's not a degree to get qualified in an examination. When the police aren't able to extract the secrets in a normal way, they torture the person mentally and physically. How far it can go, you could have understood if you would have seen Pranab. Leave it! There is no point in blaming them. Our police department has inherited it from Britishers and has added new techniques to it.

Shrikumar was listening. He was stunned. He said in a democratic government, can a person be subjected to torture just to extract the things? Before he could complete his sentence there was a roar of laughter. Shrikumar saw that all of them were looking at him as if he is an animal from the zoo. The person who was drawing the map stopped drawing, the young ladies who were busy doing their work looked at him and laughed.

His co-traveler laughed and said -Please don't mind doctor! The use of the word 'democratic' is the reason for this laughter'. India is a strange country- here in the name of Democracy the businessman adulterates the mustard oil and the shopkeeper sells colored water in the name of medicine. To save democracy an engineer and a contractor divide the profit among them and file a tender. We are a group of people who is out of this vicious circle of democracy that's why the word 'Democracy' is a matter of laughter for us. Ok, my name is Chinmaya Chakrovarty rest of them are Ka,Kha,Ga,Gha,Uaa andCha(Letters in Odia language). These three ladies are Talbai Saa, Dantae Saa, and Mrudhen Saa(Phonetics in Odia)

Chinmaya Chakrovarty! Shrikumar has heard and read this name many times. A landlord from Madinapur- after completing his Bar at Law degree from the United Kingdom, he was in a high position in the Bengal government for a few days and was a renowned constitutional expert. There are very few lawyers in India who have earned a good reputation and are renowned at such a young age. Why is he staying in such an unhygienic condition in this mountain range of Mahendra Giri in the border of Andhra and Odisha! What's the dream that they nurture for which they have left their family, name, and fame? He was surprised and astonished.

Mr. Chinmaya asked -Do you have the habit of smoking'?

"No, no I don't smoke but, where is Prasanta?"

He is there- Sleeping in that bed.

Shrikumar was surprised as he didn't see the bed on the other side. The bed was just stuck to the wall. From a distance, it looked as if a few bed sheets and blankets were dumped on it. There was no way to find out that a man was sleeping there. Other than that their callous attitude and behaviour made him think that Prasanta was somewhere else. He took out his stethoscope and hung it around his neck and said, someone please show the light. Let me see.

A young man took the Petromax light and showed. Chinmaya Chakrovarty went along with Shrikumar and lifted the bed sheet.

Is he Prasanta? Shrikumar looked at the man lying on the bed. He was a thin man stuck completely to the bed. He had a thick long beard on his face and was wearing a half sleeve vest and a pajama (A loose-fitting trouser with a drawstring). Shiv Kumar touched him, he had a high temperature, almost 102degree Fahrenheit. Chinmaya called him and said- Prasanta, Your friend, the doctor has come. The patient opened his eyes and kept on staring. His lips started quivering. A lady standing at the back made him drink water from a tumbler. He drank the water quickly and slept again.

Shrikumar was looking at him raptly. Chinmaya said -The bullet pierced him below his knee. That night the wound was covered with a cloth dipped in Benzin and the blood flow stopped. Prasanta was able to walk though he was limping. After that, we changed the place frequently and he didn't tell anyone that he was suffering from intermittent fever. Now for the past four days, he has a high temperature. He can't open his eyes and see.

Shrikumar said gravely- The bandage on his leg has to be opened. Warm some water on the stove.

One of the ladies said in Bengali- Water is kept on the stove, shall I bring? Shrikumar removed the bed sheet and saw that the bandage was dirty, and it has become harder as it soaked blood and Benzine and had dried. He took out the knife and scissors from his bag and washed it in the warm water, wiped it with cotton, and then cut the bandage with it. The patient screamed, 'Oh'! He wiped the wound with spirit. The wound has become sore. He pressed the wound from both sides and a little puss and blood oozed out from it. He applied medicine and bandaged it with cotton and gauze. The syringe was already sterilized beforehand. He took out an injection from his bag, broke it, and was ready to inject it in Prashant's body with a syringe. Chinmaya was very carefully watching Shrikumar. He said Chinmaya-Please hold his hand, he may shake it'. Shrikumar wiped the left arm with the spirit and injected and while washing the syringe he said- Nothing else to be done tonight. Let's see what can be done in the morning. The wound has become septic, maybe the wound is gangrened. It wasn't taken care of. Shrikumar washed his hand and sat on the bed.

Chinmaya's face became grave. He said- The situation was different on that day. We had to face ten armed policemen. We lost two of our comrades. Somehow we managed to get out from there with Prasanta because of Nageswar Rao. In a dark night, in that thorny forest, carrying him on his shoulder and covering a distance of nine miles wasn't possible for anyone.

Shrikumar looked at Nageswar Rao- he was none other than his co-traveller, who was walking behind him with the bundle of wood on his head and an axe on his shoulder. In the meantime he was busy cooking something as a vessel was kept on the stove. Next to him someone was sitting and chopping potatoes and vegetables with a knife.

Chinmaya Chakrovarty said -Nageswar Rao was a

lecturer in Political Science in a college at Vijaywada. He is an alumnus of Jawaharlal Nehru University. I met him there for the first time.

This type of discussion and the atmosphere was strange for Shrikumar. He sat on the bed silently. Ten years back during his college days, he met Shankar and Prasanta. He recollected the fond memories of his adolescence and youth.

Chapter-3

Prasanta Mahapatra's house was almost 10 to 12 miles away from his house. When Shrikumar finished his schooling from the village Minor school and came to Bhadrak High school for studies, he met Prasanta. At that time, Prasanta's father was SDO in Sundergarh .At Bhadrak, in his house were his grandfather, grandmother, and a servant. Prasanta was staying with them and was studying in the school. Shrikumar's father was a clerk in Bhadrak Tahasildar's office. He was shy right from his childhood so; he couldn't be together with his friends and have fun. Shrikumar had gone through the hardships in his life which usually meagre salaried family; children go through during his studies. At home, he had his parents, two brothers, and three sisters. Whatever little amount his father saved despite the difficulties got exhausted in his two elder sisters' marriage.

He has seen many times his father hiding in the house when he sees a Kabuliwala on the streets. So, to have good food and clothing wasn't in the fate of Shrikumar. Prasanta's house was near the school. During break time he went many times with Prasanta to his house and had breakfast to his heart's content. Prasanta's grandparents liked him a lot, sometimes if he doesn't go to their house; they send their servant to call him. His father sometimes insisted him not to go as it's not good to maintain close relationship with wealthy people. His mother retaliated and said-They like the boy, so they invite him sometime to have some food, why are you unable to bear it?

Overall Shrikumar knew that Prasanta is a boy who belonged to a wealthy and well to do family from his behavior and his food habits. In his childhood sometimes he envied Prasanta, but as Prasanta was courteous, he could never leave his friendship. Both of them passed the Matriculation examinations in the first division. Shrikumar's father wanted to speak to the SDO to recommend him so that he can get a job in Tahasildar's office as a clerk. Prasanta gave the money and got him admitted to a college. Both of them studied Science but after completing ISC Shrikumar got a scholarship and took admission in a medical college. Prasanta continued with his BA with Political Science Honors.

While studying in the college Shankar was a close friend of Prasanta and Shrikumar. Shankar was liked by the teachers and students as he was a brilliant student. The most alluring thing was the gestures that he made while giving a speech. His speech was powerful, radiant, and evolving, it could leave a deep impact on the listeners. Shankar Nair's father was a Kerali businessman. There were many branches of his business in Balesore district. Right from the days when he was a student Shankar had an inclination towards politics. He studied many books and fascinated his friends with the valuable information and examples from authentic resources and books. Prasanta was influenced by him.

Shrikumar was deeply in touch with Shankar for the first one or two years after he joined the medical college. Slowly he engrossed himself in his studies and his profession. Sometimes when he met Shankar or Prasanta there was only a casual conversation between them. On the other hand, the financial status of his family had deteriorated. His father retired and went back to the village. It was difficult to manage the house with his meager pension amount. So, he went on borrowing money from the village moneylender narrating him his son's bright future as a doctor. In the meantime whenever he went to the village for two or three times his father took him to the moneylenders. He couldn't understand after meeting him whether they felt relaxed regarding the loan repayment or not but he never liked it. To keep his father's reputation intact, he showed respect towards them, spoke to them sparingly.

During his father's death, Shrikumar wasn't at home. Sometimes he went to the college though he had already appeared for his final examinations .He had never imagined that his father will expire suddenly. After all the rituals were over he found out that he doesn't have the capability to run the house smoothly. All his actions were limited to the thoughts of managing the house. Before deciding any further course of action he started private practice in the village. Whatever he was earning from that was very less. First of all the villagers were scared of medical treatment, secondly to buy medicines, and to pay the doctor's fees they didn't have enough money. In the meantime Shankar and Prasanta visited him in the village. They stayed there for a week. At that time Shrikumar noticed that his friendship has slipped out of his hands.

Sometimes there was a discussion between them regarding politics, literature, social norms, and religion. On the back yard of the house his father had made a cement platform under the dense Spanish Cherry (Baula) tree.

During summer, the three friends sweep the platform and sit on it till late in the night and get deeply engrossed in their talks. Shrikumar sometimes participates in the discussion. The discussion is usually initiated by Shankar regarding the people's revolt in different countries in the world and the state of Democracy in India. While doing the scientific analysis regarding these issues there is a sparkle in Shankar's eyes and Prasanta is enthralled listening to it. Sometimes in between Shrikumar slightly objects. The content of his objection is–regarding the society, the way Shankar describes Economics according to the mathematical rules, doesn't entice him.

All the economic rules and material science rules don't fit in the context of human beings every time. He tries to make him understand that .As a doctor, Shrikumar knows that though there are simple rules for the treatment of a person, it varies according to the extremity and receptivity of a person. So, according to his view, whatever is applicable for the people of the society of Chilly, Mexico, or China that mayn't be acceptable in Indian society. But his objection is blown away by Shankar's arguments and examples.

After their stay in the village for two to three days, Shrikumar realized that his two friends didn't come to the village to console him or for their entertainment. They are involved in some type of revolt; he couldn't get the eyelet on it. Shrikumar asked Prasanta-he was about to say, but Shankar restricted him.

He said, doctor- The human society can't be rescued by revolt or movement. People like the poet, writer, musician, doctor, and engineer have to play a pivotal role to bring change into society. It's better if you remain as a doctor and don't have contact with us, you can do many things. Your responsibility towards family is more than us.

I don't want to drag you into this. May be in India in another two to five years world strategy mayn't be implemented. To sculpt the farmers, workers, and the people in the lower strata of the society into revolutionaries, we have to move ahead with many hurdles and restrictions. If it's possible, and we are alive, we will again meet in that new environment. At present our roads are different and this is preferable. Shrikumar first huffed at this blunt statement of Shankar but later on, he understood that Shankar reasoned his responsibilities towards his family and has excluded him from this igneous path.

Chapter-4

Shrikumar didn't have any attraction for a government job. His father wanted him to do a government job and to prosper, and to ultimately become a civil surgeon. But after his father's death, he decided that he won't do a government job. After a few days, he read in a newspaper that there is a position of an assistant doctor vacant in a Missionary hospital in Koraput's tribal area. The salary wasn't that bad and accommodation was available. He immediately applied for the job and got an appointment. In the village, the money lenders frequently reminded him to clear the debt. He sold the little property that he had and cleared the debts and took his mother and his younger siblings and left for Koraput.

The Missionary hospital was located in the forest surrounded by a few Kandha and Paroja tribal villages, 50 miles away from Koraput city. Villages here weren't like the villages in the plains. They were situated below the mountains, in the small lowland valleys, among the beds of Barley, Finger millet, and Yellow lentils (Arhar) and there were only 4 to 5 houses. In this place, the patient never thinks that it's necessary to go to the doctor rather doctor comes to the patient. There is no such facility of good roads. Twice in a week, the newspaper arrives by post. Still the dedication of the Missionary doctors surprised him. His hidden desire to serve mankind was self- illuminated. Among the simple tribal people he completely devoted himself to the treatment of the patients.

Usually, the people of the tribe like Kandha, Gadaba and Paroja are very hardworking and tolerant. Whenever he went to their villages for their treatment, he was baffled by their simple life and extreme poverty. They spend all their earnings on paying the debts. At least two to three members from each family work in the moneylender's house as peonage to pay their debts. Though according to the law, it's prohibited, a simple tribal couldn't take advantage of that. The moneylender threatens him; he leaves his children in his house as peonage. These things perturbed him. Many times he had been to the police and the magistrate seeking help. Sometimes they help. But for them, these are regular and everyday affairs so Shrikumar could never get a solution to this problem as per his desire. He was now in the evil eyes of two to three money lenders.

In between through the newspaper or from a discussion he came to know about the armed movement in Madinapur, Chikakol, Gopalbalabhpur, and Naxalbadi areas. Though he didn't get any message from Shankar or Prasanta still he thought that they were involved in this type of movement. In Koraput there was not much effect of it. Shrikumar was busy treating the patients so he didn't pay much attention to it.

During this time he was introduced to Sundar Das. Sundar Das's house was in Gujarat and he came to Koraput as he was associated with the Vinoba Bhave's Bhoodan Movement. During his visit to Koraput he noticed the plight of these tribals and started the first phase of Sarvodaya Movement with them. After his introduction with Sundar Das he was attracted to him. He was impressed by his boldness and truthfulness. Sometimes he discussed with him regarding the ways to help the tribals. Sundar Das sometimes stays in his house. Though Sundar Das was elder to him, a bond of friendship developed between them because of his heartiness and promptness. As per the Dandakaranya project, in Koraput, among the displaced people of West Bengal and the tribals, Sundar Das introduced many formative programmers'. Crores of rupees were spent by the government for constructing houses, for farming lands, roads, and schools for them. But a major chunk of it went to the businessmen, contractor, corrupted officers, and the politicians.

Sundar Das was firmly against it. He brought this theft to the light and headed the organized protest with people. People liked him, some were scared of him and few of them tried to remove him from their path. He was attacked twice in the dark forest, but Sundar Das was very firm in his decision. Though he was 58 years old, still in that age, he had lots of strength in his body and was also mentally strong. Shrikumar was his main associate and follower in all his work. He dedicated himself to work right from the establishment of the evening school to the movable dispensary.

The well water looks clear and transparent from the outside, but when one gets inside the well to clean it; one can find the slime and mud, broken bucket, bricks, rocks,and broken rope. It's surprising to see these things because it's unbelievable that the water which looked so transparent had some much of dirt underneath. How was the water of the well used as clean water? After being closely associated with the tribal community Shrikumar's eyes opened. He had lots of faith in social law, indissoluble trust in democracy and he wanted to work at his level. When he saw how the tribes of Kandha, Gadaba , and Paroja were tortured, his faith slowly dwindled. The problem was intense, deep rooted, and he felt helpless. At that time the only person whom he could count on was Sundar Das.

Sundar Das had lots of self confidence and faith in the nonviolence movement. Shrikumar had abhorrence towards violence and murder but, sometimes his young mind revolted- he thought nonviolence is the weapon of weak people. Sundar Das laughed and said- Doctor, not only you but many in this country, many highly qualified and learned people said this to Gandhiji. But he has proved many times that in actuality only a weak person resort to violence. In Nua khali amidst the violence, he preached nonviolence, how many armed revolutionary could do that? Those who criticized him were surprised to see that Gandhiji gave his life like a brave person when he was shot but never left the path of nonviolence. That's the mantra of Sarvoday Movement. If one can leave the fear, then there is no need of violence. We aim to establish a non violence society in India, which is free from fear. Sundar Das's words inculcated hope and inspiration in Shrikumar.

The volunteers of Sarvodaya worked in different fields with various plans. Sundar Das was associated with many people. Their opinion and ways were different, but because of the beneficial work that he was doing in the country attracted many towards him. Once he told-Doctor! Do you know Shankar Nair? Shrikumar was surprised when he heard Shankar's name from him. He asked-Where is he? Sundar Das said, he met him in Dandakaranya in a colony. He is a laborious young man, but his course of action is different from us. Shrikumar said-I know him, he is my childhood friend. They aim to initiate a revolutionary movement with the farmers and laborers of the country .Sundar Das said-that's right, there is only one way in their thought process. Rest all are deluded. Shrikumar said-I know. That's why after spending so much time in discussion and arguments; we concluded that we both differ in our opinion. But I respect his personality.

One day around 2 am, Shankar reached his house. There were two young men along with him. He said -I saw your house, if suddenly I require anything, I will send you a message. You should come immediately. Shrikumar asked him about Prasanta. Shankar said -Prasanta is with me. If it's feasible, he will meet. But don't forget what I said. When I will call you, you should come immediately. Of course, if not required I wouldn't send you any message.

Shrikumar said- What is your requirement with me? Shankar smiled and said-Brother, you know very well that we believe in Vastuvada. We don't know how to change our minds. That's why police and the punks of the moneylenders are in search of us in the forest like a hunter searches for its prey. If we fall sick, from where can we get a doctor for the treatment? That's why I expect at least a little help from your side as a friend.

Shrikumar said- Will the medicine by a doctor following nonviolence work on insurgents?

Shankar said-There is no reason to doubt-medicine is materialistic-it will work.

Six months after this incident, an unknown young man came and gave me a letter. The letter was written in a hurry. It was written-Prasanta is unwell. Come quickly-maybe a small type of operation is required.

Shrikumar couldn't go on that day as there were no doctors in the hospital. There were three to four very critically ill patients so he sent a message to go later on. He received another letter after two days-From Vijayanagaram to Jadupudi station- Govindpur is at a distance of 3 miles-come by the passenger train and reach by evening. Someone will be waiting for you. Prasanta is very sick-come quickly. After reading this coded letter he told the person bearing the letter that he will travel the next day. In between, two of the doctors joined their duty. He made some arrangements in the house and left for Govindpur. He was disturbed as Prasanta was very sick. He kept a few medicines, cotton, scissors, knife etc for an emergency in his bag .Prasanta had helped him a lot and he could repay that by treating him, this hope was there in his psyche.

Chapter-5

Shrikumar was sitting on the bed. He was noticing others doing their work unmindfully. Chinmaya Chakravarty was looking at the newly drawn map. Nageswar Rao was still sitting near the stove and was busy in cooking. The two ladies were kneading the dough and were ready to make chappatis.

Chinmaya Chakravarty folded the map and looked at Shrikumar. Maybe he wanted to say something-Shrikumar said-How will the revolution materialize, which you all are dreaming of staying away from the society in the forest? How will the public be benefited from this?

Chinmaya Chakravarty said-Doctor, we don't want to do any favor to the society otherwise we would have started constructing the Missionary hospital or night college.

Shrikumar was hurt and said – Leave the things regarding me-Is a revolt possible leaving the society behind? Other than that there must be something behind for the benefit of the society.

Chakravarty said-No Doctor, you have mistaken the true definition of revolt. The meaning of revolt is which is permanent or constant- the human society is crunched in a cobweb and is suffocated –It has to be destroyed. Then only a new foundation can be laid on an open ground easily.

The society of India has comatose- there are no mobility and progression. There are superstition, notions, and traditions existing for a long time like a cobweb. We want to abolish these. There is no place for reconciliation or compromise.

Shrikumar felt it a little awkward. He said-Hasn't the rigidity of Indian society been stamped out because of the struggle for freedom movement which continued for half a century against British rule. It wasn't possible to reform many revolutionary.

. Chakravarty said-Mr.Shrikumar,in a slimy pond, water lettuce, lotus, and water lilies are intertwined. At the beginning of the rainy season when there are thunder and shower. Maybe that time the water lettuce floating on the surface is displaced from its position-but the water lilies and lotus which are deep rooted in the slime, do they get displaced?

Due to struggle for the freedom movement; the white-skinned authority, white businessmen made the black-skinned authority and businessmen understand their way of accounting so that their capital and profit don't get ruined and are looked after properly and the black-skinned authority and businessmen could enhance their capital and business. Indians belonging to the higher strata of the society, who were trained in the UK and America about republic, socialism, and technicality applied it in their respective fields. When did revolt take place? Leaving aside the countable learned people,the rest are crores of silent general masses, who silently listened to the speeches of the politicians and in day to day life slog hard but don't get the right due. Is there any revolutionary change in their lives?

Shrikumar protested and said-After independence in 1947 there are lots of changes. Didn't the people cast their votes in the five elections, which were conducted? Their elected representatives have formed the government in the assembly and parliament.

Chinmaya Chakravarty said- Maybe you aren't able to understand what I mean to say, doctor. We don't want minor changes and enculturation, we want a complete change. In India who rules over the 100 crores population directly or indirectly? Other than the parliament there are government and opposition parties, officers, doctors, and engineers-altogether nearly 60 to 70 lakh. They all belong to the same category-almost one percent. These opportunist people have made 99 percent of the rest of the masses as puppets in their hands. This one percent is police, army, jail, and the authority who order for hanging till death. That's why those who raise their voice against them can't live peacefully even in the forests. Our aim is to disintegrate the hegemony of these one percent of people.

Shrikumar said-But government and opposition-their political agenda-election campaign-is there no difference between it?

Chinmaya Chakravarty laughed and said- Have you ever read it carefully? You will come to know that those are only empty words, nothing other than that. Whatever differences and resistance is there between them is only for power.

Shrikumar said-maybe you are right to a certain extent, but for the welfare of the tribes, there are so many projects-especially in Dandakaranya.

Chakravarty interrupted and said- Have you ever kept a dog? The tamed dog guards his owner's house without sleeping. When the owner sits on the chair at leisure and eats biscuits and cakes the dog stands, makes sounds, and wags his tail. The master sometimes throws a piece of biscuit –the dog pounces on it to eat. The government's, tribal, and marginalized community upliftment plan is similar to that. From that minister, officer, contractor, and engineer take their share and whatever is left is received by the helpless tribal people. In India, there is one third of tribal people and these tribal and the marginalized community people are deprived of their rights. The prosperity of modern Indian society is based on this profit. That's why we have started the revolt in this grass root level of the society.

Shrikumar was feeling restless. He said- India is a big country; it has a rich cultural heritage and age- old religion- Is it nothing for you other than superstition and diminishing moral values?

Chinmaya Chakravarty said- Why not anything? It is evidence of a series of persecution and injustice. Do you know what I feel when I look at the pyramid of Egypt, the temples of India, and the Pagoda of Burma and Indonesia? I see the sweat, blood, and slavery of lakhs of innocent workers which the silent history has hidden within it. You must know about the epic Ramayana and Mahabharata. SudraSamuka dared to meditate like Brahmins and that's why God's incarnation Lord Ramachandra killed him to protect the cosmic law and order (Dharma).Brahmin guru Dronacharya asked the tribal boy Ekalabya to give his thumb finger and made him disable. Belalsen and Ghatotkacha weren't born from the Aryan mother that's why the Aryan warriors killed them tactfully before they could fight in the Mahabharata war. Whenever anyone from the marginalized and deprived community is attracted to light, the so-called high society people don't hesitate to wipe out them. This is a truth which prevailed two thousand years back and also at present. The only difference is in the procedure.

Shrikumar said- But since ages, India has enlightened the whole world by its cosmic law and order. The cosmic law and order (Dharma) is the soul of Indian civilization- How can you deny this?

Chakravarty said- I am not denying, but my perception is different .Underneath Dharma, repentance and darkness have made the Indian society handicapped. That's why this society is strengthless. In the name of Dharma the astute illusionist has been fooling people for ages. The scheduled tribe people are away from this that's why they are with us in this revolt.

Shrikumar sat there like speechless-He was confused because of the argument. He wasn't able to get an answer to his justification and wasn't able to appreciate this argument.

Chinmaya Chakravarty said-Doctor you aren't able to accept what I am saying because of your preconceived notions which are there within you for years. Leave the things that you have mugged up like a parrot and try to confront the truth- you can yourself perceive that. In the deep sea, there is an animal called Octopus-it has 10 to 12 tentacles. When the prey tries to escape from one of its tentacles, it catches hold of it with its other tentacles-finally when the prey gives up it kills it. The caste system, religion, language, sacrament, and regionalism-these are like the tentacles of an Octopus. They have dominated Indian society in such a way that even if one is able to escape from one or two situations gets trapped in another. We have a firm faith- A free man is above all these. He can destroy it and that's why we are imagining a new reformed society.

Shrikumar said-Your new society is also abided by

certain rules and regulations-It will also become old one day.

Chakravarty said- Once someone asked Karl Marx-wouldn't there be any mistakes and errors in your Marxist society? Marx replied that-I can see the mistake and errors in today's society and I am trying to change those. To bring a change in the society in the future, depends on the present society. We have taken the responsibility to reform the old society.

Shrikumar said- Only to break? If you don't have any intention to create anything new then what's the benefit of breaking it?

Chakravarty said- Why not any intention to create? Let's leave the topic of creation and destruction and have chappati. You are tired, take a rest.

All of them sat in a line on a mat. A lady started serving. The arrangement was very simple- Chappati and dal cooked with some vegetables. Shrikumar was hungry- he ate with a lot of satisfaction.

Chapter-6

Shrikumar woke up suddenly. It was almost half past two. He turned around and sat. There was total silence everywhere. He couldn't make out where he was. Slowly he remembered the incidents that happened last night. He looked around. There was a small lantern which was lit up in the house but there was no one around. He stood up and walked towards Prasanta's bed. He held his hand and checked. He didn't have a fever, but his clothes were drenched in sweat. Shrikumar wiped his face and forehead. He took out his shirt and fanned him with a thick paper.

Prasanta uttered a few words. He gaped at him. Shrikumar took water from the pot and gave him for drinking. He gulped the water and again slept.

Where did they all go? When did they go? When he went to sleep Nageswar Rao was sleeping next to him with his axe behind him. He slept soon so couldn't make out where others slept or they went somewhere. Is there any other camp nearby?

He went near the door. He tried to push the door slowly but it didn't open. The door was closed from the other side with a stone. Possibly, to avoid any wild animal to enter the room. He pushed the door from inside, but the stone didn't move. He continually went on pushing from inside. He thought if someone is guarding outside may open the door and come. But no one came. The stone slowly got displaced and the door opened. Shrikumar came outside the house.

The moonlight was scattered outside. In the silent forest, in the moonlight, in the wee hours, he stood and looked around. His eyes got accustomed to the darkness; afterwards at a distance, he could see the light. He could see a narrow walking road extending till the place in that moonlit night. Maybe these people go and sit there sometimes. He closed the door and blocked it with the stone, but he couldn't muster his courage to walk to that place in the dark night. Still, he couldn't resist his eagerness. He took the small torchlight and proceeded.

After walking for a little distance, he felt as if someone crossed his way. He looked around attentively, but couldn't see anyone. By his time he had almost covered 100 meters. After walking for another 50 meters he slowed down his pace. In the forest, at a place, there was a large rock on which was kept a Petromax light covered from both sides. In the bright moonlight, he saw almost 15 people –including ladies and gents sitting together. Shrikumar could recognize Chinmaya Chakravarty from a distance, but couldn't recognize others. Shrikumar was standing behind the bushes and was thinking whether to proceed further or not and at that time he heard Chakravarty's voice.

Chinmaya Chakravarty was saying-There are few specific complaints regarding you. You need to give a justified answer. You know very well that the discipline of the party is very clear and strict. Shrikumar couldn't hear to who was the question asked and what was the reply. Maybe there is some discussion regarding the internal matter of the party and they don't want to discuss it in front of him. Probably because of that, they left the camp and came here. He thought it's not wise to walk further in this situation. He quietly stood behind a bush and was eager to listen to their conversation.

Chakravarty said- The flour mill owner of Chikakol Mr. Kuppu Swamy, adulterates the white flour with tamarind powder and powdered stone. You were made the In charge to raid his house. The party had issued him an extermination notice, but you only brought the cash, tied Kuppu Swamy, and left him unhurt. In the central jail, at the cost of the life of two soldiers, you could have got 50 rounds of bullet, but while collecting 40 rounds of bullet, when they woke up you backfired and left. There is strict instruction not to keep any relationship with the labor front right revisionist in Dandakayanya. You have pushed the most reliable comrade into their hands. You have to give a proper justification for all these. A revolutionary party can't work as a social democrat with a simple approach.

Shrikumar couldn't see the person against who were the allegations, though he very keenly observed them standing behind the bushes.

"Lastly, it's about Prasanta's sickness. The comrades were against calling the doctor to the camp. We discussed this thrice but you raised the topic again and again with the plea of Prasanta's sickness. Despite of the reluctance of the party members the doctor was brought to the camp. Do you know if we leave this camp once we have to relocate to Madhya Pradesh? On Andhra –Odisha border except for this camp all other camps are in police records. In this type of critical situation do you have any explanation for this type of activity, Shankar"?

Shrikumar was startled. He came to know that the accused was Shankar and because they had lost their faith in him so they didn't allow him to meet Shrikumar. He was upset after knowing that, to bring him to the camp was one of the allegations. He couldn't muster his courage to step forward.

Shankar replied- Prasanta isn't only my friend but a true comrade of the party. To save his life is our duty. You know that we don't have any reliable doctor and at this stage, while taking him to Chikakolam there are chances of being caught. After considering all these aspects I thought it's wise to bring Shrikumar here.

One of the ladies said- If someone would have followed the doctor or if the doctor betrays us?

Shankar said-I know the doctor very well. His perspective and our perspective may be different, but he isn't a betrayer.

Chinmaya Chakravarty said- No one is born as a betrayer, Shankar. A person who doesn't believe your philosophy can't be your friend- Chiku Bhora's this statement is completely true. Do you have to say anything regarding the complaints against you?

Shrikumar waited eagerly to listen to Shankar's answer. He suddenly remembered about third degree regarding which Chakravarty told him in the evening. They might be thinking that if the police want, they can gather information from him. Regarding this Chakravarty told him indirectly.

Suddenly someone patted on his back and said –Good morning Dr. Das. Shrikumar turned around like a lightning. In that patched darkness he could recognize the person standing next to him,he was DSP Vhaktavastalam.

Before Shrikumar could say anything Vhaktavastalam told him in a feeble tone- Slowly doctor, a little bit of noise will put our lives in danger. Of course I have a few people around, but at present, I am not ready to take any action. Shrikumar sat silently.

Chapter-7

Shrikumar knows Vaktavastallam. He is a young IPS officer. His house is in the Chikakol district. Though his mother tongue is Telugu still he speaks Odia fluently. He took birth after independence; his police department is the first protector of a Republic country. He has zeal and zest to carry on his responsibilities. He is the In charge of the task force, which was created by the combined effort of Andhra and Odisha government to catch Naxalites .He had discussed many times earlier about the Naxal movement with Shrikumar. The tribal people are sympathetic towards the Naxalites because they are the victims of money lenders, liquor shopkeepers, and landlords. He hates the moneylenders and landlords. In his field of work he has tried his best to help the poor and needy people lawfully. He doesn't trust the old style of threatening. As a dutiful government official, he is reticent. He inspires and appreciates Shrikumar as he renders his service in the villages of the tribal area.

Almost two years back when the Naxalities were murdering the landlords and money lenders in public, addressing them as the enemy of the poor class, at that time to catch or to identify the murderers enough support wasn't rendered by the general public. On the other hand, the police employees in the lower category helped the moneylender for their personal gains or due to political pressure. Due to this, the tribals didn't trust them. Finally, the accumulated change into distrust and hatred. The general public in the villages weren't Naxalites but, those who were the victims of the moneylenders and lost their land and house for a meager amount of money were benefitted by the work done by the Naxalites. The mortgaged property documents were burned in the presence of the public, some of them got back their land which was occupied by the money lenders and few could get the food grains like rice, finger millet and corn during the plunder. The Naxalites when raided the money lenders house they seized the stocked wheat, sugar, and finger millet, and distributed it among the people. In brief for ages the tribals and the villagers who were scared of the money lenders, landlords, or police, the work of the rebels changed their perception. That's why people adored the Naxalites. All of them informed the Naxalites about the plans of the police except those whose family was troubled.

Slowly there was a confrontation between police and Naxalites. Mostly for the guns and bullets they attacked the police station. The government's work process is usually slow; there were raids in both Andhra and Odisha but there was no coordination between the governments' of these two states. The Naxalities raided in the Andhra region and easily moved into Odisha .Andhra police weren't able to trace them out. Sometimes they raided in Odisha and easily moved into the Andhra region. Due to this reason after the discussion in a high level meeting of the authority, with the help of both the state governments a special task force was formed and Vakavasthalam was entrusted with the duty to head it.

After taking over the charge of anti- Naxalite task

force Vhaktavastalam was in search of the camps of the rebels in the forests and mountain areas situated in the border of both the states. He along with one or two sergeants or sub inspectors searched in the forests and mountain range. Slowly information was gathered about them from various people. Vaktavastalam analyzed each information very carefully and took further action accordingly. He knows-those who are operating this movement –the masterminds involved in this were equally educated and intelligent like him. They have sacrificed their lives for a political disagreement. A small mistake may cost a life that's why he takes each step very carefully and cautiously .He knows that if they are taken as criminals and convicted there are chances of been getting defeated.

Chikita is a small block on the border of Andhra and Odisha. To travel to Chikita through the national high way one has to go through Andhra. This type of border areas has Naxalite base camp. Vhakatavastalam got the information two weeks back that from Chikiti, 20 kilometers away in the base of Bodagiri mountain in a tribal village few unknown people was seen. A letter packet arrived in the village in the name of Lachana four days back. The post peon was going to deliver the packet to Lachana. Lachana was a peon in a minor school and in his name were sent few English magazines and letters from Calcutta. The post peon became suspicious. Lachana hardly receives one or two letters in his mother tongue in his school address. But getting a registered parcel isn't a common thing. The post peon asked Lanchana and he replied that his cousin works in Calcutta and now he is in the village and the packet has come to him. The post peon's brother was a constable in the police station. He told his brother regarding this and his brother told it to the police In charge. The police In charge instructed the home guard to secretly keep an eye on Lachana. The home guard came after two days and reported that at a distance from the village Lachana has a pearl millet field. He stays there in a small hut to take care of the crop. Now few people have come and are staying in that hut. Few of them have seen Lachana taking food items for them. The In charge officer reported this to Vaktavastalam.

One day Vaktavastalam went alone to that village. The home guard was informed secretly regarding it beforehand. Vaktavastalam along with the home guard went to the pearl millet field. The field had a fence. He stood near the fence and looked at the house carefully. The house was made up of woven palm leaves. It was closed from three sides and open on one side. He saw that there was no one in the house and a small child was looking after the field. He suspected as he saw a blouse was kept for drying on the woven palm leaves. The tribal women generally don't wear blouses. Vaktavastalam wasn't in his police uniform. He dressed himself up as a common man in a loincloth and a shirt. He called the child who was in the pearl millet bed and asked him where did Lachana go? The child said that he had been to school. Vaktavastalam asked when will the crop be harvested and did Lachana sell the bed to anyone?

Generally, tribal people sell the crop or the bed to the money lenders before harvest. The child thought maybe a money lender wants to purchase the pearl millet and searching for Lachana. Vaktavastalam walked down towards the house which was in the middle of the field. He saw that there was a movable stove. There was nothing else in the house. He saw that there were two English newspapers tugged on the roof. The newspaper was printed in Calcutta and was almost a week old. He left the house.

On that day he came to Ichapur and gathered almost ten constables and two officers. He called the Chikita police station In charge and asked him to be cautious. Around 10 pm in the night, Vaktavastalam took a station wagon and travelled towards Chikiti. He reached near Lachana's pearl millet field and posted two constables to keep an eye. All of them had guns. Vaktavastalam took out his pistol, took others, and entered the field.

At that moment two men came out of the house through the open door. They saw the police party and screamed-Be alert. Then from the house, there was continuous firing. The two men who were outside fell as the bullet hit them. The rest of them made an escape from the back. The sub inspector who was near the door was hit by a bullet and he fell. Still, he fired and the bullet struck one of the man's legs who was running away. The sub inspector saw him limping and walking for a short distance. Vaktavastalam chased the rebels for some time but they ran towards Bodagiri Mountain. Vaktavastalam came back and asked an officer to search the house and ordered to send the two injured Naxalites to the police hospital. The bullet had pierced the chest of one of them and he was bleeding profusely. The other one was almost dead as the bullet hit his head.

Vaktavastalam again followed them after giving the order. He had five armed soldiers along with him. But because of this half an hour gap, it wasn't possible to trace them. He searched in the bushy forest for 3 to 4 hours but it was in vain. He went back to Ichapur , ate a little, and left for the police hospital. He saw that one of them was already dead and the other one was about to die; two ribs were broken and the bullet had pierced his heart. It was a surprise that he was still alive. Despite of all the efforts in the hospital, he died in half an hour.

Among the dead one was Lachana, who was the other one Vaktavastalam couldn't recognize. Only from the tailor's label at the back of the shirt, he came to know that it was stitched in Calcutta's New Abhimanyu. So he suspected that the dead man belonged to West Bengal. He sent the two dead bodies for postmortem and left for his office. The dead man's photograph was sent to Calcutta police for identification.

Chapter-8

After Chikiti encounter though Veaktavastalam tried to find out where did the Naxalities go, but he couldn't. He went to many places to search according to the information of his newsagents but wasn't successful. He thought that the man who was injured must be under treatment in a nearby hospital. All the nearby hospitals were informed to report immediately if any patient is under treatment who is hurt by a bullet. But there was no report from anywhere. He finally thought that maybe the wound wasn't so deep or maybe there is a doctor among the Naxalities who might have been treating the person secretly. Few private doctors who had a soft corner for the rebels, their clinics were under watch by the police. Still, there was no news.

The day Shrikumar got down from the train and travelled towards Govindpur, the information was conveyed immediately through telephone from the railway station to Ichapur police station. At that time DSP Vaktavastalam was in the police station and he reached the station in his jeep. Three hours after Shrikumar left the station, Vaktavastalam along with the sergeant and the three soldiers marched ahead in the same route. It was difficult to follow the footsteps in the narrow forest path, after walking for a few distances he thought that the group which was walking ahead might have changed their route. After inspecting here and there he reached near the small river.

There was no way to cross the river so he entered the channel with the pistol and torchlight in his hand. One of the sergeants kept an eye on the front part of the river and Vaktavastalam along with two soldiers entered the river. There was little water in the river, but the flow was intense. But it wasn't so difficult to cross it. On the other side of the river, he could see some faint footsteps. The road wasn't smooth, it was filled with thorns and there was also a chance of being attacked. He walked ahead very cautiously. After travelling a distance he could see a dim light in the forest. He concentrated on the light and moved ahead. At night the tribal people to chase away the wild animals lit the fire in their fields. He thought maybe they have reached a field. After walking for a while he saw the house. From a distance, he tried to assess the geographical state of the place. Then he instructed two of his companions to go to the backside of the house and wait.

Two hours after Vaktavastalam reached the place he noticed that the door opened and eight men and women came outside and sat on a rock. The rock was almost 300 feet away from the house. They had a Petromax light, but it was covered from two sides so only the light was falling in one direction.

Vaktavatsalam saw- All of them went and sat silently on a rocky platform. Maybe they were waiting for someone. After some time three young men came from the other side of the mountain .It seemed as if the person in the middle was guarded by the other two on both sides. After they came and sat the discussion between them began.

Vaktavashalam was almost 50 feet away from the house and was hiding silently behind a bush. He wasn't able to hear everything which was being discussed. As he was between the house and the rocky platform .He couldn't keep an eye on either side.

Slowly the discussion was at a high pitch so he could hear a little. In between he looked towards the house; he had the fear that he may be suddenly attacked. At that moment the door of the camp opened, Vaktavastalam noticed that someone stealthily walked towards the lighted rocky platform. He could make out from the activity of the visitor that he wasn't interested about the place of discussion, but was curious to know, what was being discussed.

He crossed Vaktavatsalm but couldn't realize his presence. From the activity of the person in that dim light, he could make out that the person was none other than his known, doctor of the Koraput Missionary Hospital, Doctor Shrikumar. It immediately stuck to his mind-The doctor might have been brought there to treat the man who was injured in the firing the other day .He thought that the information that he got about a visitor who came by the evening train for which he travelled such a long distance maybe the doctor. As his companions were on the other side of the house and as he couldn't communicate with them so he couldn't confirm.

DSP Vaktavastalam from his previous conversation and discussion with the doctor knew very well that he doesn't believe in the violent act of the Naxalites.

He is a devoted coworker of Sundar Das. Why is he here then? Is it so that the doctor is meeting them in secret! Otherwise why he would have come here! Maybe the doctor had some personal or any other type of close relationship with the injured person. Many questions arose in his mind but he couldn't come up with a justified answer to all these questions. As they left the doctor in the camp and as the doctor was stealthily trying to listen to the conversation, it was clear to him that the doctor doesn't have any connection with their party; because of necessity, he might have been brought there.

He thought- Can the doctor leave unhurt from that place after their necessity was fulfilled? That's why he made up his mind to let the doctor know about his presence, but he may panic, so he took the necessary steps.

Chapter-9

Shrikumar was startled when he saw DSP Vaktavastalam. He could never think in his dream that police can be so close to the Naxalite camp to check on their activities. What was discussed wasn't audible.

For two to three minutes there was silence, then Chakravarty said-Do you have to say anything?

Shankar stood up and said-I hate killing people unnecessarily. I think because of the unnecessary killing of people we are moving away from the mainstream. They don't like the unessential killing of people. Other than that, the two constables in the police station belonged to the lower middle class family and to make their living they are working. If they would have been killed their family would have become helpless, it wouldn't have shaken the foundation of the government. I believe now it's time to again discuss this issue in the party.

Chakravarty remained silent for some time. Then he slowly said-We have worked together for a long time Shankar. Today your philosophy and the philosophy that the party follows are different. To achieve the goal, we should be stern and firm. There is no place for emotion or disagreement in this case. Here we kill to show our potential and insurgent in front of the common people. For this, why only two constables, even a true comrade's life can be sacrificed.

At that moment, the sound of a stone rolling down from the opposite direction of the rocky platform where the discussion was going on could be heard. Nageswar Rao stood up immediately and the Petromax light was extinguished. There was a sound of the bullet being fired and someone said in a low voice-Enemy run! Shrikumar was perplexed. Vaktavatshalam pulled Shrikumar towards the bushes. There was the sound of frequent exchange of fire and after some time the bright ray of the torchlight was focused on the rocky platform.

After 10 to 15 minutes, the firing sound slowed down. Vaktavatshalam took out the whistle from his pocket and blew it twice and lighted the torch as a signal. After some time a sergeant and three constables came to him. The sergeant said-I am sorry sir, we were hiding behind the rock .Without our knowledge, a stone tumbled down and created the noise. Before we could reach, they started firing, extinguished the Petromax light, and escaped into the forest in that darkness. I thought it wouldn't have been wise to follow them instead of coming back to you. The sergeant's leg was bleeding as it was wounded because he was hurt by the stone. He had tied the wound with a handkerchief.

Vaktavasthalam along with them walked carefully towards the camp. They placed Shrikumar in the center. They had the apprehension that there may be an exchange of fire there. In sign language, he told all of them to wait 50 feet away from the camp and walked alone towards the camp. After five minutes he lit the torch and signaled others to come.

Shrikumar entered the house and saw that all the things in the house were deranged. He looked at the papers and books piled up on the table in the night and found most of the things missing. Vaktavastalam posted two constables at the backside of the camp and started searching. There were few rugs left on the bed. He shivered as he thought about Prasanta who wasn't in a good condition and how dangerous it is to take him away in this dark night. He felt obliged towards Nageswar Rao. Maybe because of him, he will remain alive. If they would have left Prasanta, then Vaktavastalam would have sent him to the police hospital and later on, he would have been interrogated and sent to court. Chinmaya Chakravarty's firm words resounded in his ears-At the time of necessity, if required the life of a true comrade can be sacrificed.

Vaktavastlam and his companions were collecting all the paper, including the small torn bits of paper, and were tying those in bundles. Shrikumar was sitting on the bed and was looking at their activity. After an hour when everything was arranged and tied Vaktavastalam said-Let's go. The three constables collected the bundles and started walking. Shrikumar followed them silently.

Shrikumar and the police party reached near the small river. On the other side of the river, there was a jeep and three police officials. They took all the things and kept in the jeep. Shrikumar sat in the jeep with Vaktavastalam.They started their journey towards Ichapur.

It was almost dawn by that time. The twittering of the bird in the forest and the glow of the horizon was creating a mesmerizing scene. Shrikumar was silently watching it. They reached the police station early in the morning.

Shrikumar knew-He will be asked many questions. The trained interrogators will apply their scientific skills and question him to collect all the necessary information.

He wasn't stuck with terror because of that. In his subconscious mind, the scintillating experience of the previous night was lingering. He closed his eyes peacefully. He dozed sitting on an armchair which was on the porch. It was a reawakening day.

Chapter-10

Shrikumar was unaware that he slept in that chair. When he woke up, he saw a constable sweeping the porch. He opened his eyes and couldn't immediately realize where he was in this unknown environment. Slowly he recollected the incident that had happened the previous night .He took out a glass from his bag and asked the constable for a glass of water. It was almost 7 am. Shrikumar saw that DSP Vaktavastalam was sitting near the table. He was in the same dress that he wore the previous night. He was busy writing something on the paper and the papers were piled up on his left side on the table. He saw Shrikumar and said-Good morning Dr. Das. You have slept for almost two hours. Have a cup of tea.

Immediately two cups of hot tea were served. In the meantime Shrikumar had washed his face and brushed his teeth. He had a cup of tea and then asked in a sharp tone- Mr. Vaktavastalam are you going to detain me? You may arrest me also.

Vaktavastalam laughed loudly and said-No, no, why should I arrest you? Whatever you have thought regarding the police, we don't do that much of unlawful work. There is no such valid reason or complaint against you. Other than that to visit a wounded friend or to treat him is a normal thing, that's why I think that you haven't committed any crime, but if you have any other type of association with the Naxalities then that's a different issue. If you are in way connected to them then definitely you wouldn't publicize it. Unless and until we find out anything regarding it according to our system, till then you are out of suspicion. Still, there are few things about which I am not clear regarding last night. I hope that you will help me with this.

Shrikumar said briefly-You may ask. Vaktavastalam smiled and said-Not now. You have taken a rest for two hours, but I couldn't rest even for a second. I will have bath, take a rest, and speak to you in the evening. I think you won't hesitate to be my guest for a day?

Shrikumar thought that there is no way to refuse .He couldn't understand how has the incident taking a turn. He looked at Vaktavastalam, stood up, followed him, and went and sat in his jeep.

Mr. Vaktavastalam's quarter was in the police line a little away from the police station. The jeep halted in front of his quarter. Two small children- a girl aged 7 years and a boy aged 5 years came out of the house and wished Shrikumar. Vaktavastalm took his son by his arms and hold the hand of his daughter and went inside the house. Shrikumar followed him.

The living room was very clean. There was a sofa set with two chairs. Next to each chair, there was a side table. The doors and windows had curtains, and on the table cloth, there was an oriental painting. In the corner of the room, there was a book rack. Two photographs were hanging on the wall. One was Vaktavastalam's photograph in training college and the other one was a family photograph. On the other side of the room, there was a tall vase with colorful flowers.

Shrikumar was sitting in the living room and was noticing all these. Vaktavastalam came along with his wife and sat on a chair near Shrikumar. Vaktavatsalam's wife Meera was the daughter of a Navy officer from Waltair. She is a graduate. She could understand Odia, though she wasn't able to speak .She wished him in English. She was holdings two plates of snacks. A servant came and kept a glass filled with water. Mrs. Meera Vaktavastalam sat down and said in English-I heard that you were awake the whole night, so you must exhaust. Have some snacks and take rest .I will wake you up before lunch.

Shrikumar liked and appreciated the behavior of Mrs. Meera. The apprehension that he had in his mind was almost cleared now. Vaktavastalam didn't speak anything and started eating with lots of enthusiasm. After some time he drank a glass of water and said-Oh! I was very hungry. Doctor, no one can be compared to our Indian ladies when it comes to feeding anyone.

Shrikumar wanted to make the discussion a little pleasant and said-I don't have the privilege to know this.

Vaktavastalam said-I think you have hidden this information from everyone otherwise every day in the morning at least half a dozen brides' father would have queued up in Koraput's dense forest region. After my IPS I couldn't go out of the house in the morning and in the evening because of these brides' fathers. That's why one evening I decided that I will select a girl and in the morning I saw Meera Devi at my door. I caught hold of her and tried to hide under the hem of her saree.Where could the brides' father find me? Vaktavastalam laughed loudly cracking this joke. Mrs. Meera showed false anger and said- As if I got the information that Mr. Vaktavastalam is looking for a bride and to protect him from the bride's father I landed up in the morning. All Rubbish! She said-If you say, I can look for a bride for you.

Shrikumar folded his hand and said-Excuse me! I am a doctor in a Missionary hospital. I don't get a chance to do private practice. I am staying in the forest region-I could hardly manage my living with the salary that I get. I don't have a house of my own-why do I need a wife (Gruha Lakshmi)?

The atmosphere became pleasant with the hearty laugh of all. Vaktavastalam took Shrikumar and showed him the restroom and went for taking a bath. Shrikumar took out the towel from his bag and went inside. There were a new soap and a tub filled with water in the bathroom. He took his bath. After taking a bath, he combed his hair, changed his clothes, and felt fresh. In the meantime Vaktavastalam's servant served him a cup of coffee. While Shrikumar was drinking his coffee, Vaktavastalam entered the room along with a gentleman. He said, Doctor, he is one of my friends, Paresh Mahapatra-a police official of the government of Odisha. He was on his way from Paralakhamundi to Berhampur and suddenly his vehicle broke down. He came here. I thought-let me introduce him to you.

Apprehensions and doubts peeped in Shrikumar's mind .He said-Please sit down Mr. Paresh.

Paresh Mahapatra said-I am also a student of Bhadrak College like you. But when I joined, by that time you had already left the college. We have heard your name from the teachers in the college whenever they cited the example of brilliant students.

Shrikumar looked at Mr. Paresh for a while. He said-Mr. Mahapatra, I don't know what you have heard about me, but, I don't believe that you suddenly stopped here on your way to Berhampur. Mr Vaktavastalam knows me for the past 3 to 4 years- I have a good relationship with him.

That maybe the reason, he will find it difficult to ask me few undesirable questions.

Mr.Paresh interrupted in between and said- No, no, Mr Vaktavastalam is an officer of Andhra government. In the task force against Naxalites, both Odisha and Andhra officers work. I am in the police department of the Odisha government and I am associated with the task force. I know you .Whatever information we get regarding this issue is discussed between us. We know that you aren't associated with the Naxalites from the information that we have gathered. But, as we saw you in the Naxalite camp, we think that you have got an opportunity to be with them for some time. So, to get some information from you regarding them is quite natural.

Shrikumar said-You may kindly ask me whatever you want to know.

Mr. Paresh said-What's the reason for bringing you here? Through whom were you given the message? Do you know anyone who is associated with the Naxalites in your Missionary hospital or from the nearby area? Shrikumar said-I neither know any Naxalite in Koraput, nor do I have any association with them. My friend is associated with them. I got the information regarding his illness and came here to help him in his treatment. It's quite usual that they don't go for the treatment in the government hospital as they are scared of people like you. I got the message through one of my other friends. But, I don't want to disclose the name of this friend. Mr. Paresh said-If I am not wrong the person who gave you the message is Shankar-Shankar Nair and your sick friend is Prasanta Mahapatra.

Shrikumar was astonished .He said-How do you know? Mr. Paresh giggled and said-Not through astrology. I have just now come from Koraput after visiting your dispensary. Shankar Nair met you almost two months back.

We know that both Shankar Nair and Prasanta Mahapatra are associated with the Naxalite movement and they were your friends when you were studying in Bhadrak. Shrikumar said-Then, there is nothing for me to hide.

Mr Paresh asked-Who are the other people? Who are they? What's your relationship with them?

Shrikumar narrated the incident right from the moment he got down in the station till he was back-except what he had discussed with Chinmaya Chakravarty regarding the rebellions .In between, Mr. Paresh was noting down a few things and was asking him a few questions.

In the meantime Mrs. Meera came to ask them for lunch. Mr. Vaktavastalam and Mr. Paresh also joined him for lunch. All of them had their food silently. Then Mr. Vaktavastalam said- Doctor if you want, you may leave for Koraput, but as you can recognize Chinmaya Chakravarty and Nageswar Roa that could be a threat to your life. We may sometimes need your help. Please! Be careful.

Shrikumar said-There may be a threat to my life, because of that I can't just hide. How can I help you? I am not associated with their movement, but if I meet any of my friends, do you expect me to report to the nearest police station immediately? Rather, you can arrest me or can punish me according to the law. But, I can't do what you want.

Paresh Mahapatra looked at Shrikumar for a while and then said-There is no reason for arresting you. Whatever information we needed, we got from you. If required, you will be again called.

Shrikumar didn't say anything. Mr.Vaktavastalam took him in his vehicle and left him in Ichapur station. There was some time left for the East Coast Express to arrive. Shrikumar booked the ticket and sat in a secluded corner of the waiting room.

Chapter-11

The train arrived and Shrikumar went and sat in a second class compartment. The compartment wasn't overcrowded. Just a few minutes before the train could leave, a bullock cart arrived in the station. From the bullock cart, a woman clad in a Burkha, an elderly Muslim gentleman, and a man who had wrapped himself in a bed sheet got down. Shrikumar was looking at the platform through the window. The elderly Muslim gentleman had a white beard on his face, wore a cap, was dressed in a white pyjama, and a black coat. He held the hand of the other person as if helping him to walk.

It seemed the man was sick or wasn't able to walk properly due to some reason. The man had beard, a turban on his head and was completely covered in a bed sheet. He was leaning over the Muslim gentleman and was walking. Behind them was the woman clad in Burkha. They came and stood near the compartment where Shrikumar was sitting. The gentleman said in a firm voice-we will get into this compartment. He opened the door and helped his co-traveler to get into the compartment. There weren't many travellers in the compartment. A hawker who was selling groundnut got into the compartment from Ichhapur-maybe he will get down somewhere in the nearby station. There was another traveller who was already there in the compartment. The Muslim gentleman kept his bag on a vacant seat, took out a bed sheet from it, and spread it on the vacant seat. He took his co-traveler and made him to sleep there. The Burkha clad woman sat near the feet of the man who was lying down. The Muslim gentleman said-Salim, I am leaving now.He went near the Burkha cladded woman and said-Please be careful. He got down from the compartment and left. Shrikumar was silently looking at the platform. The guard blew the whistle and showed the red flag as the signal and the train started moving slowly.

Though Shrikumar was looking outside, still the incident that happened the previous night was lingering in his memory. Right from the meeting at midnight on the mountain till the time he reached DSP Vaktavastalam's house, he thought about all the incidents. There was only one question that was bothering him-What's the condition of Prasanta and where he would be? On the other hand, he was also anxious about Shankar.

The difference in opinion among the insurgents often ends with the bullet. Maybe taking the advantage of the darkness, someone who belongs to Chinmaya Chakravarty's group might have tried to kill Shankar. They might have thought that the arrival of Shrikumar and then the police were preplanned by Shankar. The way the things happened so quickly, it's obvious that someone will suspect, Shrikumar agreed to this. They might have thought that Shrikumar is associated with the police.

DSP Vaktavastalam brought Shrikumar with him, kept him for the whole day in his house, if any closet reporter of the Naxalite group would have been following him, then this kind of suspect is usual. DSP Vaktavastalam dropped him in the station in his jeep- considering all these aspects; there is enough reasoning that he has a close association with the police. Therefore when he was leaving, Mr. Vaktavasalam informed him that his life is in danger.Of course, that mayn't be impossible. Shrikumar was perplexed. He is not a timid person- he wasn't able to determine how and in which way to prevent the danger to his life. He again thought-Is it a plan by the police to give them information regarding the Naxalites? Is there any hidden motive behind the favorable behavior of DSP Vaktavastalam and Mr. Paresh?

When he was engrossed in his thoughts, he was startled by the touch of someone. He looked back and saw-The Muslim Burkha clad woman had removed her Burkha. She said in Bengali –Hello! doctor. Are you going to Koraput? Shrikumar looked at her in surprise. The face was a little familiar-but he couldn't recall where did he see her. The lady said-Did you recognize me? He looked in surprise-she was the same lady who was along with the Naxalites the previous night and was helping him when he was examining Prasanta. He was bewildered and said-You? Here?

The lady replied in Bengali- After yesterday's raid, it wasn't possible to take Prasanta far away from there. Others left-But I and Shankar took Prasanta to the mountain cave and sat there for the whole night. We had noticed that the police had taken you-but, you will escape so easily from their clutches was beyond our imagination. That's why after seeing you in this compartment Shankar told us to sit here.

Shrikumar asked -Shankar? Where is he? I didn't see him!

The lady said-the Muslim gentleman- who made me sit here was Shankar. I think you weren't attentive that's why you couldn't recognize him .After seeing you, he told us to get into this compartment. Shrikumar asked-Is

Prasanta with you? The lady replied-Yes, he is sleeping there. Of course, because of the injection that you gave he doesn't have a fever since yesterday. Right from the morning other than drinking water, he didn't eat anything.

The speed of the train slowed down. It was about to reach Palasha station. The lady again wore the Burkha. Shrikumar put his hand beneath the bed sheet and checked the pulse of Prasanta. He didn't have a fever-but, the pulse rate was slow. Maybe Prasanta became tired as he had to walk through the platform.

The train stopped at Palasha station. Shrikumar got down and arranged for bread and milk. He took the help of the lady to lift Prasanta. Prasanta sat down with a lot of difficulty .Both of them made him eat two slices of bread dipped in milk. Shrikumar had brought some snacks for the lady.He gave her that to eat and he had a cup of tea.

The train left the station and caught its speed. After three hours Shrikumar will reach Vijayanagaram station. He will take a bus from there and go to Koraput town and from there he has to go 50 miles away to reach the Missionary hospital. It wasn't possible to take Prasanta there in present condition. He is physically unfit and can't go there. Shrikumar was angry with Shankar.He didn't do the right. He brought Prasanta in this condition and left him on the train. Later on, he thought- What can Shankar do? Maybe this is the only way to rescue Prasant from the clutches of death. Shankar himself isn't free from danger. He will think of a way out for himself if any arrangement can be done for Prasanta .

The lady saw Shrikumar sitting engrossed in his thoughts and she asked- What are you thinking doctor?

Shrikumar said pensively-I am thinking, at present where Prasanta can be taken?

Can you take him along with you? the lady asked. Shrikumar said- I don't have any problem taking him, but, how will he get down from the train, travel by bus till Koraput, and then cover a distance of 50 miles till the hospital? His condition isn't good and I can't gather my courage to take him. If we can get a taxi, then it's possible.

The lady said-My uncle works in Vijayanagram. He is a well to do contractor there-I have decided to take Prasanta there for the time being. Till he recovers, I will be there with him. After he recovers the further course of action will be decided.

Shrikumar felt a little bit relaxed. He said, at least for taking rest and treatment he can avail the facility. Are there any chances of any danger there? The lady laughed and said-Is there any place where danger isn't there? I am travelling with you on this train, if suddenly any danger comes then how can you help me?

Shrikumar became shy and said-That's right, whatever you mean by help for that, I think I don't have the intelligence and capability. Leave that topic-That day while talking when I asked Mr. Chinmaya he tried to avoid telling me your name. I hope that you won't have any problem now telling me your name? The lady said- My name is Shrilata Banerjee. Shrikumar said- How did you come to know Shankar and Prasanta?

Ms.Shrilata looked around the compartment carefully. In the meantime, many travelers were there in the compartment. The hawker who was selling groundnut was sleeping, keeping his head on the load that he was carrying. Few of the travelers were Odia speakers and a few of them were Telugu speakers. It was almost 2 am and most of the travelers have slept and a few of them were dozing. It was summer-towards the dawn it was a little cool inside the compartment.

Shrilata covered Prasanta with a bedsheet and said-That's a long story; in brief, I can only say that I was not connected to them regarding any political matter. At Kolkata in the labor colony-where, Shankar and Prasanta were working with other laborers for trade union work, at that time I met Prasanta during few cultural programs. A group of young men and women had created a drama group named 'Agragami' based on their contemporary outlook . I met Prasanta and we became close. My father is a chartered account in Calcutta and he earns well. I was doing my post graduation in Social Sciences at the University of Calcutta.I met Shankar several times near the university coffee house. They recruit the party workers based on their ideology, I came to know about it very late. Sometimes I think whether I have complete devotion towards their political work or not.She remained silent for a while and said-Whatever it is I have been with them for a long time. I think my future is with them. I don't have time to think anything else.

Shrikumar said- You are all highly intellectual people-How much experience do you people have regarding the life of crores of daily wage workers and regarding the farmers? To bring a change in a dream, other than a hope; you don't have the opportunity to see it closely. Therefore, whatever you think, you can do for them; they mayn't have faith in it. Those who are ruling now, they also had a dream like you to bring the changes. They mayn't have succeeded-but--

Ms.Shrilata smiled and said-After Prasanta recovers you can discuss it with your friend regarding this. I have already told that I have psychological apprehensions regarding this issue. We have almost reached .We have to get ready to get down.

The train slowly arrived at Vijayanagram station. It was almost 4am.As the train arrived the empty platform became crowded. Shrikumar and Shrilata woke up Prasanta. He looked at Shrikumar's face with empty eyes. Both of them held him and slowly got down on the platform.

Ms.Shrilata said-I have sent a telegram to my uncle from Ichapur. Someone might have come.

At that time, at a distance, a well dressed gentleman was seen looking at different compartments of the train and was walking. He wore an expensive suit and was almost 54 to 55 years old. He was holding a fanciful stick. Shrilata saw him and said-I am here uncle. The gentleman stopped. Ms.Shrilata bowed down and touched his feet. To introduce me she told-Uncle, he is doctor Shrikumar Das, a friend of Prasanta, and he is Prasanta. She looked at Shrikumar and said-He is my uncle-Sandeep Banerjee.

Mr.Banerjee felt a little uncomfortable. His niece who was highly qualified was dressed very simple, was along with sick Prasanta who was in his dirty clothes, and Shrikumar in his Khadi clothes-all these seemed a little weird to him. Still out of courtesy he said-Good morning everybody. The driver of Mr. Banerjee was standing behind him. Without him, it would have been difficult for Shrikumar and Shrilata to make Prasanta to cross such a long platform. He almost lifted and carried Prasanta. Shrikumar walked along with him till the car which was outside the platform. Mr.Banerjee and Shrilata were walking behind them. Shrikumar made Prasanta lie down in the car and sat with him. Mr.Banerjee and Shrilata sat in the front. The car moved ahead.

After ten minutes the car stopped in front of the porch of a big three storied building. Shrikumar opened the door and got down. A Gorkha watchman came and opened the front door of the car. Mr.Banerjee and Shrilata got down from the car.

On the front door, it was written 'Banerjee Mansion'. Shrikumar got down and told Shrilata-I will take a leave now.I have to take the bus to Koraput.

Mr. Banerjee said worriedly-No, no how can you leave immediately! Take a little rest. There are so many buses to Koraput during the daytime.

In a tender voice Ms. Shrilata said- If you don't have any problem doctor, then please check up Prasanta once in the morning. You have come for him.

Shrikumar couldn't say no. The driver and the guard held Prasanta and took him to the guest room on the ground floor and made him lie down on the bed. Shrikumar sat down on the chair and looked around.

The guest room was expansive. There were two beds with Dunlop pillow mattress. It was covered with a clean bed sheet. There was an attached bathroom. In the middle, there was a round table with three chairs. There was a sofa and a side table in one corner of the room. Shrikumar went to the bathroom, washed his face, and brushed his teeth. He felt a little fresh. Prasanta was sleeping. He covered him with a bedsheet.

At that time the guard brought a cup of coffee and asked- Sir, do you need anything else? Shrikumar drank coffee and gave him back the empty cup. He slept on the bed in the dim bed light.

Chapter-12

D octor! Please get up. It's 9 o'clock now. Shrikumar woke up at the call. Prasanta was still sleeping on the bed. Maybe the bedsheet slipped from his body at night, as it was a little cool so he was sleeping with his hands and legs together. Shrikumar hurriedly went and washed his face in the washbasin, wiped his face with a towel, and opened the door.

Shrilata entered the room with two cups of tea on a tray. In the meantime, she had already taken her bath. She was dressed up in a very simple way. The apprehension and worry had made her face look stern last night, but at present, there was no sign of it. She was looking youthful. She smiled and offered him a cup of tea and made a gesture to wake up Prasanta. Shrikumar took the teacup and shook Prasanta to wake him up.

Prasanta twisted his body and woke up. He leaned on the backrest of the bed and looked at Shrilata and then he looked around. ShriLata offered him a cup of tea. Prasanta took the cup, but instead of drinking the tea, he gazed at ShrLlata.

Shrikumar said-Prasanta, please have your tea, then we will explain to you about the changed situation. Do you remember travelling by train yesterday night?

Prasanta as an obedient student drank the tea and

then asked in a faint voice-Where am I now? Where did you come from?

Shrikumar laughed and said-We are now in the guest room of Ms.Shrilata's uncle who is a wealthy businessman. As you are unwell, as your doctor of yours I am also enjoying the hospitality of him. Shrikumar laughed and said, if you recover quickly we will be deprived of the hospitality.

Ms.Shrilata said- No, no doctor. On behalf of my uncle, I commit you that you can stay here as long as you wish.You can at least stay until your patient gets well.

After drinking tea Prasanta tried to stand up and go to the washbasin to wash his face. Though he didn't have fever still he was weak and because of the wound on his leg, he was staggering. Shrikumar held his hand and took him to the bathroom. Prasanta washed his face in the bathroom and then came and sat on the bed. Shrikumar took out his toothbrush, toothpaste and shaving kit from his bag and went to the bathroom.

After half an hour he came out of the bathroom after completing his daily routine. Shrilata was sitting on the chair and Prasanta was leaning on the pillows and laying down on the bed. In between, they drank two more cups of tea. Both of them were silent and serious.

Shrikumar said Prasanta- You may go to the bathroom quickly and finish your daily routine. I am very hungry. We will have breakfast together when you come back. After that, I will do the dressing of your wound. Prasanta got up from the bed.There was a new towel kept on the bed rest.He took it and walked limping towards the bathroom.

After Prasanta left, Shrikumar told Shrilata-Today Prasanta's health condition is much better. Though he doesn't have a fever, still he has a weakness- after taking rest for a few days, he will recover .

Shrilata nodded her head in an unacquisitive way. After some time she said-Prasanta didn't like coming to my uncle's house in this way. But I didn't have any other way.

Shrikumar said-Yes-If that would have been done-means if he would have been left in the cave, he wouldn't have survived to argue. Leave it. I will try to make him understand. The blind followers of philosophy and socialism think in this way.

Shrilata was irritated said-All the policy and philosophy should be understood in a broader sense keeping the goal in mind.To protect the policy and philosophy if someone tries to be suicidal then it's pointless.

Shrikumar clapped his hand in support and said-Now you are supporting my point of view.All the philosophy in the world is meant for a better and peaceful living-not for curiosity and death.

Shrilata was a little worried and she said-No, no I don't agree with you about everything according to your point of view. If a person or society proves to be cancerous, it's better to cradicate it before it spreads so that there is no chance to repent over it later on. But, that's a different issue. In brief, Prasanta thinks that for his illness to call for you and due to this the police got the information regarding the camp is the biggest mistake of Shankar. Other than that it isn't justified to be so sentimental for the life of a comrade. In Similarly we have lost many comrades in the past in the hands of death. Other than bringing him here is another mistake because of this the police will get the information and will create problems for the party.

Shrikumar wanted to make the situation normal and

said-As two minuses becomes plus, a similar way two mistakes can prove to be beneficial. According to Prasanta-It would have been better instead of calling me there, police raid and causing other problems, straight away, he should have been sent along with you to the in- laws house.

Shrilata became annoyed and said-What are you saying doctor-we don't have as such--

At that moment Prasanta opened the bathroom door and came. He had shaved his beard and was wearing a white pyjama and a shirt. He was weak and looked pale as he was anemic, but as he wore clean clothes he looked a little fresh. Shrilata looked at him for some time and then got up and left.

After some time a servant arrived with two plates of breakfast on a tray. There was bread, eggs, and fruits. Both of them had their breakfast in silence.

While drinking coffee, Shrikumar said- I heard that you didn't like it as you are brought here. Of course, when Shankar called me whether he discussed it with you regarding it or not that I don't know-maybe you weren't in a condition to discuss regarding it. But, after that till your arrival in this place-Shankar did everything to keep you alive. Of course, others knew that Shankar had sent a message to me to come. Shrikumar narrated everything in detail right from his arrival at Govindpur till Vijaynagram.

Prasanta was leaning over the bed rest and was listening to him silently. After listening to everything he said- Shrikumar,if I would have been emotional and romantic then I would have been grateful to you for what you have done for me. But, I am not thinking in that way-After so many days of hard work and planning the base camp which was set up on the border of Andhra and Odisha, was ruined because of my health issues. All the comrades were disconnected from each other, it will be very difficult to bring them together, search for an appropriate place, and set another base camp. To keep me alive, Shankar has created in convenience for the party's insurgent activities.

Shrikumar said-I have discussed with Chinmaya Chakaravarty in detail regarding your party's insurgent activities. Of course, at that time you were not in sense due to fever. Do you believe-without bullet and firing there is no revolution? Is it not possible to get social justice by following the rules and regulations of the law?

Prasanta said-The killing by the punks, dacoits, and terrorists is nothing other than brutality. But, in a weathering, junked society where there is an abundance of selfishness and disdain, to bring a radical change,the armed revolution is an inspiration for the common people. There is no value of any particular person or a group in that frame of reference- It is pointless. Prasanta stopped for a while and said-You can't understand it, Shrikumar,I am filled with guilt and remorse- whatever damage is caused to the party is irreplaceable.

Prasanta became exhausted after talking for a long time. He got up and laid down on the bed. Time was flying-Shrikumar sat on the chair and started reading a newspaper.

Chapter-13

It was almost two days. It was an afternoon on the third day. Shrikumar and Prasanta were sitting and talking on a different topic. Shrilata was sometimes participating in the discussion. It was almost four days since Shrikumar left Koraput- It will be troublesome for him if he will be late. Prasanta was also not ready to stay in Shrilata's uncle's house.

At that moment it seemed as if someone came from outside. The person who came was none other than Nageswar Rao. He was wearing relatively clean clothes and wasn't carrying his axe.

Nageswar Rao entered the room. They were astonished to see him. He said-Since yesterday evening the police are keeping an eye on this house. Anyhow Prasanta has to leave the house that day. They didn't get the proper information yet and maybe the local police have informed Vaktasatlam. Prasanta became impatient after listening to this. Nagesawar Rao told that he will be waiting for him outside and he should get ready within 15 minutes to leave the place.

While changing the clothes Prasanta said-Doctor, I am leaving now. Maybe we will meet in the future. Then he looked at Shrilata and said-Your photo or identity isn't there with Andhra or Odisha police. Maybe in the meantime, it will come from Calcutta –Be careful! I don't want to involve you anymore in this uncertainty.

Shrikumar looked at him and said in a feeble voice- You aren't well-

Prasanta smiled and said-There won't be more facility in the jail. Other than that I don't have a fever now. If I would have taken a rest for some time, that would have been fine. But, there is no other way.

Shrilata arranged a few clothes for Prasanta in a bag. She kept a bread packet, a tin of biscuits, boiled eggs, and bananas in the bag. She only said-Eat something on the way.

Prasanta asked-Are you going to stay here for a few more days, Shrilata? It will be safe for you to go back to Calcutta.

Shrilata replied-I am thinking to go to Koraput along with the doctor and stay there for a few days if he doesn't have any problem.

Shrikumar said-There is no problem. I have a small house-maybe you will face some difficulties. Suddenly he remembered the house in the forest and his stay over there. He said-It will be good. It will be better if you come-you will get an opportunity to know the difference between the work that we are doing for the tribal people and the work that you are doing for them.

Prasanta said-There is hell and heaven difference between your work and our work. We prepare them as revolutionary warriors and you! Ok! Shrikumar I take a leave.

Shrilata and Shrikumar came to the door. There was a rickshaw in which Nageswar Rao was sitting. Prasanta went and sat with him and the rickshaw starting moving.

Shrilata and Shrikumar came back to the house.

Shrikumar said-Shrilata, now I don't have the responsibility of Prasanta. It will be better if we leave tomorrow in the morning. Shrilata said 'yes' and went inside the house.

It was evening. Shrikumar thought of going out in the evening to move around the city, but after Prasanta left he didn't feel like going out. He started reading a few English magazines.

It was almost nine in the evening. Sandeep Banerjee along with Vaktavastalam and Paresh Mahapatra entered the room. Sandeep Banerjee is a known contractor and also a wealthy person that's why he knows the higher police officials. Paresh Mahapatra looked at Shrikumar and said-Doctor I doubted that you are in Vijayanagram as you didn't reach Koraput. Maybe any of your friends might be there.

Mr. Banerjee left the police officers to make some arrangements for the guests. After sometime cashew nuts and coffee was served and then came Shrilata .

While serving coffee to the police officers Shrilata said-I am Shrilata Banerjee and Sandeep Banerjee is my uncle. I do the research work in Calcutta. Dr.Shrikumar Das is my friend. Do you want to know anything else about me? I met Dr. Shrikumar at Vijayanagram station and I requested him to stay back as I want to go to Koraput with him.

Shrikumar understood-Shrilata doesn't want to give any information regarding Prasanta. She said- Before returning to the Koraput Missionary hospital, I stayed here to enjoy the rich hospitality.

Vaktavastalam was looking at Shrilata very keenly as if he was trying to recollect something .Paresh Mahapatra said-That's good-the doctor belongs to my village, so he is my friend. I got an opportunity to make friendship with you. But, what's the reason for going to the forest area of Koraput?

Shrilata said-I only know about the forests and the primitive tribes of Odisha by reading the books. While researching in sociology, it's necessary to have real life experience and knowledge because it will help in many ways. So, it won't be wise to miss this opportunity.

Vaktavastalam said-I think I have seen you before somewhere. Of course not able to recollect where did I see you.

To make the situation a little bit easy, Shrikumar said-Maybe in the market or in the train. God has gifted Shrilata with beauty so you might be thinking that you have seen her before.

Mr. Paresh said-We got the information that you are staying here. We thought to meet you again. We take leave now .Both of them got up and left.

After they left Shrilata took a deep breath and said-It seems, they didn't get any information regarding Prasanta.

Shrikumar said-It seems like that. Maybe they didn't see Prasanta here so didn't ask about him- but nothing can be said with certainty. The way Vaktavastalam looked at you I thought he—

Shrilata thought for a while and then said-We will leave for Koraput tomorrow morning. My uncle is a businessman, it's better not to bring him into the vicious circle of suspects.

The cook brought food for Shrikumar. Shrikumar washed his hand and sat on the chair to have his food. Shrilata went inside the house. Shrikumar sat quietly on the bed. After Prasanta left, he felt that his presence wasn't necessary in the house. For the past few days he was in an unknown and bizarre environment, today he is free from that. He looked out through the window at the moonlit night. He was surprised as Shrilata showed her interest to go to Koraput.

He couldn't understand her intention behind it. Is she interested to be in contact with other rebels those who are there anonymous or to set up a base camp there is pre-planned? Did she discuss this with Prasanta? If it is so than for Shrikumar the situation will become worse. Will he tell her not to go on any pretext? Finally, he decided that he will act according to the situation. After deciding, he slept.

Chapter-14

It was almost a week after Shrikumar and Shrilata reached Koraput. In the absence of Shrikumar there were alternate temporary arrangements made for the patients, now to treat them is his responsibility. Other than that, a doctor's duty in the Missionary hospital doesn't get over by only examining the patients and by writing the prescription. He has to go regularly and visit the distant villages and check whether the patients are treated properly and are recovering or not. Shrikumar finishes his work in the hospital by 12 pm, has his lunch, and takes his bag, rides the bicycle, and goes to these villages regularly.

By the time he comes back, it is almost 6 pm to 7 pm .The compounder and the nurse in the hospital takes care of the hospital in the evening. At present in this area, people are mostly affected by fever. It has spread like an epidemic. Each village has 30 to 40 patients because of that the second doctor has put up a camp at a distance of 20 to 25 miles away from the hospital. Shrikumar's responsibility is to look after the patients in his area. Sometimes he returns home tired in the evening, and sometimes he has to stay back to look after the serious patients.

His mother and his siblings are aware of Shrikumar's routine. When Shrilata came to their house Shrikumar's mother was a little dissatisfied. She had many apprehensions and doubts in her mind. But when Shrilata bowed down her head as a mark of respect for her, addressed her as Maa, helped her in the daily chore, spoke to Shrikumar's siblings with lots of love and affection, she was accepted as one of the members of the family.

At times Shrikumar and Shrilata couldn't meet. If they meet, they speak just about some usual things in life, nothing more than that. In the meantime Shrilata has become close to Sundar Das. Sundar Das had formed a society called Girijan Mahila Mandal. After the formation of the society slowly the enthusiasm slowed down. Shrilata has now taken over the charge of the society. She is can meet the tribal women because of this. The tribal women usually don't do anything other than the daily household work. Shrilata's initiative has helped them to make badi, papad etc., which they sell in the market and earn some money. At present, she is planning to construct a night school for the women.

Sundar Das had enumerable power to influence and create enthusiasm in others do work. Shrilata discusses with him regarding the problems that the tribals face in their family. She was surprised as the tribal ladies were unaware of taking care of their children, they were unaware of the overall mental and physical growth of the children .Sundar Das says-What is there to be surprised? They aren't like the money plant growing in the drawing room which will wither without water and mineral.

Nature has bestowed them with an abundance of strength-if you cut any vine in the forest, it will again revive with the new leaf sprouting from it which is an indication of a new life. They are so much accustomed to life in the forest that it's not necessary to guide them at every step. The culture of city life had made life cripple .A child in a city can't step down from the cradle without the help of his parents, teacher, or siblings. But there is no question of a cradle. Didn't you hear- A thorn in the forest blooms in its own yard.

In between a supervisor came from Calcutta to inspect the work going on in the Missionary hospital. Shrikumar went along with him to different villages and explained to him how the patients could only be given a general treatment because of non-availability of modern medical equipment. The supervisor promised to provide an X- ray machine and few medical equipment and left. The supervisor had a few Bengali magazines and books with him. Shrilata couldn't get anything to read from the day of her arrival other than a weekly English magazine. So he collected those Bengali magazines and books from the supervisor.

Shrikumar returned to the hospital around 2 pm. He had his breakfast in the morning and left home around 7am.When he returned he saw, Shrilata was waiting for him without having her lunch, and his mother had been to the neighbour's house. Shrilata saw him and said, go and get freshen up, the food is becoming cold. Shrikumar washed his hands, feet, and face with water. While wiping his face with a towel he said, today a visitor from Calcutta had come to our Missionary hospital. I have got a few Bengali magazines and books from him, for you. You have become a savage as you aren't getting any books to read here. Shrilata didn't show much interest-she said-I will see later on, let it be there. Oh! You don't need those magazines and books.

Shrikumar said-I am a doctor; patients and medicine is my profession. I don't have time to read literature, about politics and criticism. To become a doctor one needs to sacrifice many things. Sometimes the battle that is fought between life and death is more thrilling than the stories in the magazine and books.

There was no provision to have food on a table so both of them sat down on a mat to have their food. Shrilata kept the curry on the stove to warm it. As she was working near the stove, she was sweating a little. She wiped her face in the saree pallu (end of the saree), lifted the pan with a tong, and brought it near the place where Shrikumar sat and served it in his plate. Shrikumar had never seen her before in this way. He gazed at her face. Shrilata said-What are you looking at? I am very hungry. Let's eat. While eating Shrikumar said-Shrilata I never had an idea that a brilliant student of Calcutta University who belongs to a wealthy family can adjust to this environment in this way.

Shrilata started eating and said-There is nothing unusual about this- you have seen, how we stayed in Govindpur camp. We were entrusted with the duty to arrange for food there. In India the social norms are such is that all the girls at least know a little regarding how to cook. Of course, those who are brought up in the western style, their case is different. She stopped for a while and said-keep the things about me aside-as you said, the battle between life and death is more bizarre than any thriller story or novel.

Shrikumar said-You must be knowing Shrilata that at present there are so many new inventions and research in the field of medical sciences so the responsibility of a doctor is more. Nowadays especially the diagnosis of a disease is done more technically. In the Soviet Union of Russian, an operation is done by an ultrasound knife, where the loss of blood is almost negligible. But in this forest region of Koraput when I have to operate in the dim light of a kerosene lamp or have to do handle a delivery case-when the patient or for his near and dear ones struggling between the apprehension of life and death, I have to stand with the ordinary instruments, am I in the twentieth century? In this place to get rid of the disease, pain, and death both the patient and the doctor rely on God's mercy.For a person who confronts this type of situation every day for him any type of thriller story is inadvertent.

Shrikumar was talking while eating but towards the end, he couldn't eat. Shrilata also stopped eating and looked at him. She said-In India the resources are very less and the population is more-any type of revolution associated with violence, doesn't matter how powerful it is, can't bring a solution to this problem. Shrikumar was elated. He caught hold of Shrilata's hand and said-You are right Shrilata, now you agree 50% with my point of view. Let's see what happens in the future. Shrilata felt shy when she saw his excitement-she was embarrassed .She said-Let's finish the food and then we will think whose point of view is right.

Shrikumar finished his food, washed his hands, and went and sat on the chair. Shrilata went into her room. Shrikumar won't go out today. There is a festival of the tribals, therefore there are celebrations in the villages. In Koraput most of the tribals are Christians but that doesn't cause any hindrance to the celebration of any festival. For them,religion means the amalgamation of the certain notions -which is unchangeable and fixed. A simple tribal man doesn't get into the complexity of religion. For ages, the notion that he has imbibed in himself, he adheres to that and thinks it as the ultimate truth.

Today Shrikumar won't go to the villages to treat the patients so he went to the hospital around 3 pm. Shrilata also went along with him to the hospital. In the absence of Shrikumar ,Shrilata had been to the hospital once or twice.

There were 2 to 3 tribal women, those who were waiting for the doctor. They had come to take the medicine for fever. One of them was holding a 3 to 4 years old boy on her arm. Shrikumar saw that the boy had a high temperature. He instructed the nurse to wipe the head of the boy with a wet towel and after that gave him some medicines. He wrote the prescription for others to take the medicine. The tribal women were talking regarding something and were laughing. Shrilata said-They don't get enough to eat properly, don't get clothes to wear, and they live in unhygienic conditions in the hut, still, how are they able to laugh? Shrikumar said-That is a gift of God.

It was almost evening. In the interior places of Koraput it gets dark by almost 4.30 pm. Shrikumar gave the instructions to close the hospital and came out. Nearby the hospital there was an open field. He went and sat on a rocky platform. Shrilata followed him, she also went and sat there.

There was half moon in the sky and the chirping of the birds was heard from the dense forest intermittently. Slowly there was silence everywhere. In the forest trail, someone was walking either with a lantern or a fire lit torch-sometimes the light could be seen. The music played with the instrument for the tribal dance could be heard. It seemed as if nature has come to a standstill. Shrikumar likes this silence therefore he comes and sits on the rocky platform for an hour or two. After some time he looked back and saw that Shrilata was sitting engrossed as if she is enjoying each moment. In the partial shadow and lighted she looked like an ascetic. Shrikumar looked at her raptly.

Shrilata broke the silence and said- Let's go. Both of them climbed down the mountain and walked towards the home.

After returning home Shrilata went to Shrikumar's

mother. Shrikumar's mother was rolling chappatis at that time. Shrilata washed her feet and hands and sat down with a chopper (Paniki) to cut the vegetables. Shrikumar went to his room. There were three rooms in the quarter and a room with a grill in the front which was a sitting room. Next to his room, there is a room where his mother and siblings stay. The last room was a children's study room, but after Shrilata came it's her bedroom. There is a bed and a cloth rack stand in that room. There is a small table on which is kept a medium-sized mirror, next to it there is a small stool. All the rooms have an electric bulb and a fan.

Shrikumar was sitting in his room and was going through the weekly English magazine. In between, he could hear his mother and Shrilata talking. Shrikumar's mother was born in Madinapur-She could speak and understand Bengali that's why most of the time Shrilata and his mother speak in Bengali with each other. While speaking with Shrikumar, Shrilata speaks in a mixed language of Odia and Bengali.

From the day Shrikumar met Shrilata he was curious to know more about her though there was no as such attraction towards her. In the beginning, he thought that there is a deep relationship between Shrilata and Prasanta-maybe they are planning to get married. Afterward he came to know about the closeness and friendliness among men and women in the Naxalite group. He understood that Shrilata was Prasanta's reliable comrade. In between, he developed an attraction towards Shrilata. Shrikumar is reserved, he speaks less; he doesn't like to be very casual and indulge in any type of fun.

He gets peace in doing his work silently. Today after coming back suddenly his attraction towards Shrilata has compounded. He thought-If Shrilata could stay with him lifelong in this beautiful forest, maybe the meaning of life will become complete. But Shrilata has come only for a few days-What's the intention behind it, isn't known. A girl born and brought up in the busy city of Kolkata can only enjoy the beauty of the forest for sometime-can she survive in the forest for life long? For Shrikumar this forest, the simple tribal people and to be a part of their life in their sadness and happiness is a life that is meaningful and veritable. It may be attractive for Shrilata-but can't be a meaningful life. He fell asleep thinking about several things.

Chapter-15

Shrikumar woke up around 10 pm and saw Shrilata was trying to wake him up. He immediately got up from the bed. Shrilata said-Won't you eat? It is almost 10 pm, children have already slept. Mother is waiting for you in the kitchen and dozing. Shrikumar got up, washed his face, and sat down for dinner. Shrilata also sat down next to him to have her dinner. After eating in silence for some time Shrikumar asked- Shrilata, can I ask you a question? I hope that ,you will give me the right answer. Shrilata laughed and said-Let me know what do you want to ask. Shrikumar said-Why did you suddenly decide to come to Koraput? Did Prasanta tell you to do that? Shrilata said-No, rather than that when Prasanta was getting ready to go with Nageswar Rao, I decided to come to Koraput.

Shrikumar asked-But why? You didn't have any plans to come to this Missionary hospital of Koraput , and the tribal villages, then why did you come?

Shrilata wanted to ignore the question and said-Is everything done according to the plan? Is there any problem with you because I came here?

Shrikumar said impatiently-No, no, rather I thought you would face problems here.

Shrilata said-Hope you don't have doubts now.

Shrikumar said-I don't have doubts regarding that ,but you answer to my question.

Shrilata ate silently. In the meantime Shrikumar had already finished his dinner. Both of them washed their hands and went to Shrikumar's room and sat.

Shrilata said-When you reached Govindpur camp, before that there were too many discussions regarding you. They suspected you before your arrival. Except for Shankar, no one was willing to trust you, and Shankar left for another camp just before your arrival. When you arrived, all of them mocked at you looking at your attire. After that, you discussed and argued with Chinmaya Chakravarty-this initiated their suspect. Though you were not a spy of the police from your arguments, it was very clear that you were against the rebels.

Despite of all these, there was one thing which attracted me towards you-That is, your admiration for life and abhorrence towards violence and killing. In your personality, there was a reflection of reverence, internality, and trust .I thought- can a life be lived with reverence and love? Listen! Shrikumar-The flames of a rebellion had extinguished the innate quality of an artist within me who love and care for the people and now it again became alive. I want to see how will be life leaving behind the violence, killing, and accepting life wholeheartedly? Shrilata was excited. Shrikumar looked at her speechless.

After sometime Shrikumar asked her slowly- Did you finish taking my examination, Shrilata? Shrilata laughed and said-The day it gets over I will give 100/100 to my student.

Shrikumar said-I apprehend Shrilata, The student on whose success you have so much of trust ,may disappoint you.

Shrilata said-If that type of dismal, unfortunate situation arises, I won't back out to say it clearly and she left for her room. Shrikumar sat silently and looked outside the window. He felt restless and after some time fell asleep.

It was around 3 am ; Shrikumar heard the noise of a gathering outside and woke up. He got up from the bed, washed his face, wore his shirt, and went outside. There was a small police van and behind it was a jeep which was parked in front of the hospital. Few police constables got down from the jeep followed by the inspector Mr. Paersh Mahapatra.

According to his instruction, the hospital was opened and three injured persons were brought in a stretcher and were laid down on the bed. Among them, one was Shrikumar's friend Shankar, there was a constable and the third one was an unknown person. Sundar Das also got down from the jeep along with Mr.Paresh Mahapatra and when Shrilata saw him, she came outside the house. Shankar was hit by two bullets on his left leg. The police constable wasn't injured badly but the other person was wounded by the bullet on his chest and the shoulder.

Shrikumar immediately got ready to do the operation. He has to operate and take out the bullet and then has to stitch the wound, otherwise due to bleeding the patient may die. The nurse and the compounder reached the hospital. Luckily, few other doctors had arrived earlier that evening and were available that's why both the patients were taken to the operation table immediately.

Shrilata came and stood near Sundar Das and wanted to know about the matter. The matter was- A tribal, whose name was Kulink was working in the Indravati Project, and had a camp. Shankar was staying in that camp. The unknown person was the chief of the laborers- his house was in Ganjam district.

For a few days he had an eye on a tribal girl. Last night the girl was returning home alone around 8 pm in the night at that time the chief of the labourers along with one of his friend's tried to molest her. Till 10 pm when she didn't return to the camp, she was searched for. At that time someone told about the chief of the labourers and he wasn't found in his house. Shankar and two other people went to the forest with the light and found the girl raped. She was lying unconscious. There was a lot of agitation in the labourer camp and all of them went to the chief's house and asked him to come outside.

The chief instead of coming outside fired two bullets with his country- made pistol. The bullet hid Shankar's calf muscle and thigh. Shankar also fired back. On that day, Paresh Mahapatra was available in the project police station. When they heard the firing of the bullet, they came to the spot. Sundar Das was also spending his night in the nearby ashram. Both of them brought the injured persons to the hospital in a police vehicle for treatment. In that chaos, a constable was also injured- though not seriously.

Shrikumar was operating the chief of the labourers. As the bullet hit on his chest, two of his rib bones were affected, but luckily the bullet didn't hit him in his heart or his lungs. A lot of blood had accumulated in his stomach. To operate on such a patient with limited available instruments wasn't easy. Luckily, few instruments had arrived from Calcutta; still the condition of the patient was critical. By the time the operation was over, it was almost 5 am. The doctor had taken out the bullets from Shankar's leg. Shrikumar was tired; he washed his hand with the soap and went to the office room. Shrilata prepared 3 to 4 cups of tea and served them.

Shrikumar had his tea and went near Shankar's bed. Shankar's leg was tied with a bandage after removing the bullets. Shrikumar took his hand and checked his pulse. If the stitches are done properly and blood flow stops then he will recover soon. He went back to the office room. Sundar Das and Paresh Mahapatra were talking at that time. In the meantime the constable was also treated. Paresh Mahapatra looked at Shrikumar and said-I may leave now Dr.Das. Both the patients are unconscious now; I will again visit in the evening. He looked at Shrilata and asked-How much are you through with your research? How long are you going to stay here?

Shrilata looked at Paresh Mahapatra intently and said- I don't work for anyone Mr. Mahapatra- I do the research work in Sociology because I am interested in that. If required I can spend my whole life here. Mr. Paresh looked at her for some time and then headed towards his jeep. He asked Sundar Das-Will you come with me? I will drop you on the way. Sundar Das smiled and said-Let's go! Both of them took leave from Shrikumar and Shrilata and left the place.

Shrikumar left for his quarter. Shrilata also followed him. Shrikumar looked at Shrilata and asked-Are you going to stay in this forest lifelong?

Shr Lata said-Don't you believe?

Shrikumar said-No, everything is possible for you. If you decide on it, I will be grateful if you don't leave my house.

Shrilata said-I will think over your proposal. Both of them reached the house.

Shrikumar took bath and had his breakfast. It was a

simple breakfast-Rice flake, sugar, and banana. He left for the hospital at 8 am and went straight to have a look at the chief of the laborers. The man was strong, otherwise, he would have survived. He wrote some injections and medicines in the prescription and gave it to the nurse and then came to have a look at Shankar. Shankar had regained a little of his consciousness. He called him. Shankar in a very feeble voice said-There is a lot of pain. Shrikumar consulted his co doctor and gave Shankar an injection and returned back home.

Shrikumar reached home and saw Shrilata standing in his room and going through a magazine. She asked-How is your patient?

Shrikumar said- A little better. Shankar may recover within a week but nothing can be said about the chief of the laborers. But, It's true that the man is strong enough, otherwise, he wouldn't have survived. If no other problem or infection occurs, he may survive but there is a chance that for lifelong he may get crippled.

Shrilata looked at him and said-Is it necessary to keep the man alive? What damage would have happened if a Hemlock like him would have got killed by Shankar's bullet?

Shrikumar said-Why did Shankar shot him?-I don't know whether to protect himself or to kill him. But I am a doctor, Shrilata-I live righteously. The aim of my life is to save the life of the people-I don't take into consideration if a person is a terrorist or a saint if he comes to me for treatment. I use all my skills and intelligence to save that person. That's the goal of my life. He paused for a while and said-Shrilata, I remember one of the sayings of Mahatma Gandhi- Hate the sin not the sinner. Who is a sinner and who is virtuous isn't listed in my duty. He said-Shrilata, it's also necessary for Shankar that, the man should survive. If that man survives then maybe Shankar will be punished according to the law, but if he dies, then won't it be a difficult situation for Shankar? As a friend of Shankar, it is my responsibility to save the life of the Chief of the laborers and hand him over to the law.

Shrilata slowly became normal. Through the window, a ray of light fell and brightened her face Shrikumar could see respect and blithe in her eyes.

Chapter-16

Shrikumar came home, had his food, laid down on the bed, and fell asleep. Around 3.30 pm Sundar Das came. Shrikumar woke up, brought him inside the house, and made him sit. Along with him came the unfortunate girl and her mother.

Sundar Das said-Doctor, I have brought a letter from the police for medical examination. Mr.Paresh will come now. After you do the medical examination of this girl and submit the report, I will file a case against the chief of the laborers and the contractor.

The girl was almost 21 to 22 years old. As she belonged to a hard working tribal family, so was physically sound. Her eyes were swollen as she cried a lot. Shrilata came and sat near the girl and asked her a few questions.

Shrikumar was in a dilemma to do a medical examination of the girl. There was no lady doctor in the hospital .Sundar Das said-You are a doctor, how can you be in a dilemma? If there would have been any requirement for your sister and if any lady doctor wouldn't have been there, then won't you have done the medical examination? Shrikumar left for the hospital along with the girl-His mother, Sundar Das and Srilata went along with him.

Shrikumar did the medical examination, washed his

hands, and sat down to write a report. Shrilata went to meet Shankar and asked the nurse about his health condition. Shankar had a little bit of temperature, so the doctor who was treating him had advised to keep him a light diet. Shrilata immediately went home and brought some bread and hot milk for him.

Around 5 pm Mr. Paresh along with the local police officer came in the jeep to the hospital. The local police officer was an experienced person and he had a lot of respect for Sundar Das. He got down from the jeep and asked Shrikumar about the medical examination report and took it from him.

Mr. Paresh went to meet Shankar. At that time Shrilata was feeding Shankar with bread and milk. Mr. Paresh asked-Ms. Banerjee, do you know Shankar before?

Shrilata said-Shankar is the doctor's friend, in that way he is also my friend. Other than that I have the experience of nursing.

Mr. Paresh asked-Mr. Shankar, can you answer to few of my questions now?

Shankar was silent.

Shrilata said- Let him recover a little. He has a temperature today. You can wait till tomorrow-after he recovers a little he can answer to your questions. Is he going away anywhere? Mr. Paresh smiled and said- Maybe you don't know him, that's why you are saying this. Of course, he can run away with his injured leg. He may not go away being in company of people like you. Mr. Paresh along with the police officer sat on the jeep and left.

Shrilata spoke to the tribal girl and her mother and consoled them. Shrikumar's mother gave them rice and vegetables to cook and eat. Shrilata gave Sundar Das Rs 100 and said that it's a small contribution from her side to fight the case in the court. Sundar Das took both of them and left.

Shrikumar went and saw Shankar and the chief of the laborers. Shankar was sleeping after having his food. Shrikumar didn't wake him up; he went to check the other patient. After checking his condition prescribed to give him glucose saline.

Shrikumar left the hospital and came home. He took out the surgery manual which he didn't read for a long time to gather more information regarding the treatment procedure. He had never performed any major operation like this after joining the Missionary hospital. According to his experience that he gained while studying in college, he operated. There was no other way at that time other than this. If he would have sent the patient to the government hospital which was 50 miles away, the patient may not have survived.

Around 11 pm in the night, the sound of a motorcycle was heard. Prasanta along with another unknown young man entered the house like a typhoon. Prasanta said-Shankar is injured. I got the message today in the morning. Where is he?

Shrikumar's mother and Shrilata came outside the house as they saw Prasanta. Shrikumar's mother was happy to see Prasanta after so many years. Prasanta bowed down his head in front of her as a mark of respect. All of them left for the hospital to see Shankar.

Shankar was sleeping. He wasn't having a temperature. Prasanta called him two to three times and he opened his eyes.

Prasanta said-I have come here to see you, Shankar. It was good that the doctor was there so your treatment could be done immediately. How many more days do you need to stay here?

Shrikumar said- At least for ten days. Of course, the bullet didn't hit his bone. Still, it will take time for the wound to get healed.

After that, all of them left the hospital and came to Shrikumar's house. On the way Prasanta said-Brother we are indebted.

Shrikumar laughed and said-I have kept an account of the interest and the principal. You both will repay it later on.

After reaching home, Shrikumar's mother called Prasanta to serve him food. Prasanta refused to have food and drank a cup of tea. After that he told Shrilata-Srilata, you may come along with me today. We will again reorganize our party.

Shrikumar looked at Shrilata attentively. Shrilata said-Please! Don't pull me again into it. You know very well that to a certain extent my thoughts are different from your party's approach. At present, I am clear about my responsibilities. I am working for the Tribal Women Society with the help of Sundar Das.I hope that you won't misunderstand me. Prasanta looked at her for some time. He said- Is this your final decision, Shrilata?

Shrilata looked at Shrikumar once and said-Yes, I have decided it finally.

Prasanta looked at Shrikumar and said-I take a leave now. You will take care of Shankar.

Shrikumar walked with Prasanta for a distance. Prasanta and his comrade left the place on their motorcycle.

Shrikumar came back home. He saw Shrilata standing near the doorway and looking outside. There was a mark of reverence and radiance on her face.

Shrikumar held her hand and with a lot of affection said-Shrilata!

Shrilata said-I will stay here for few more days, Shrikumar.

Shrikumar didn't say anything. He looked at her enchanted. The darkness was expanding outside.

Chapter-17

The next morning Shrikumar took his bath and got ready to go to the hospital. Shrilata was supposed to go to a far village on that day. She was also getting ready-She will go with the volunteer from Sundar Das's ashram. In between Shrilata had visited few villages to mingle with the tribal women and Shrilata to know about their problems .But, she thinks that she hasn't succeeded. With her efforts, a few Health Education centre has opened in a few tribal villages. Shrikumar couldn't visit those very often but, Shrilata tries to make the women folk understand and give them general information regarding how to maintain good health. She helps them when they are sick.

Before leaving for the hospital Shrikumar called Shrilata and said-You were supposed to go today. If you can wait, I will treat two to three patients and accompany you.

Shrilata said-Yes, I will also go and find out about the well- being of Shankar.

Both of them left for the hospital.

Shrilata saw that Mr. Paresh Mahapatra was sitting near Shankar's bed. There were two constables standing behind him. He saw Shrilata and asked-Ms. Banerjee, what's the condition of your patient? Did Shankar regain his consciousness?

Shrilata said-I think you can tell about the patient much better than me as you are here before me.

Mr.Paresh said-I was waiting for the doctor to come so that I can discuss it with him. Shrilata said-The doctor has already come. You may go now.

Mr. Paresh got up and left but the two constables were still standing there.

Shrilata went near Shankar, took out the sheet, and checked him. She could make out that Shankar was conscious but he was acting as if he is sleeping because of the situation. She told the nurse to bring warm water, took out the clothes from Shankar's body, and did the sponging with the cotton. Very carefully she kept Shankar's wounded leg on a pillow so that he doesn't feel the pain. She spoke into his ears and said-Shankar, will you eat anything? Shankar said very slowly-Afterwards.

Shrilata then went to Shrikumar's room. Mr. Paresh was sitting there. He looked at Shrilata and said-Please sit down, Ms. Banerjee. It seemed as if they were discussing something. Mr. Paresh said-One of our officers went to Calcutta to collect some in formation. Though we didn't get the exact information, still we were able to collect the list of the names of the teachers and students of Calcutta University those who are associated with Chinmaya Chakravarty's group. It's not that all of them are working in the border region of Andhra and Odisha. At present most of them aren't there in Calcutta and maybe through that thread, we will come to know about them. Doctor, please try to recall the names that you might have heard during their conversation.

Shrikumar said hesitatingly-I don't remember listening to any such names and I am telling you very frankly that Mr. Chinmaya very bluntly refused to give me any identification. It was obvious that they didn't trust me.

Shrilata suddenly said-Doctor, try to recall, did you hear the name of Shrilata Banerjee?

Shrikumar was baffled.

Shrilata was sitting in front of Mr.Paresh and Shrikumar was sitting behind him. Shrilata could see the expression on Shrikumar's face but Mr.Paresh couldn't notice. He laughed and said- Ms.Banerjee, we aren't ignoring any possibilities. But without getting the proof nothing can be said. Shrilata said-Then work hard, maybe you will get the result.

Mr. Paresh asked-How is the health condition of Shankar?

Shrilata said- He doesn't have a fever, but I did the sponging for a long time, don't know whether he could feel it or not.

Mr. Paresh said- I will go to the police station and look into that girl's case. He stood up and walked away.

Shrikumar went along with Shrilata to see Shankar. While going, he caught hold of Shrilata's hand and said-Shrilata, you are appalling. I would have been caught if I wouldn't have been sitting behind.

Shrilata said-I saw that you were baffled and your face turned pale. But whatever it is, whenever I see these police officers I become exasperated and speak bluntly.

Shrikumar said-Shrilata, you have formed a fixed notion in your mind regarding them; there are police officers who are well- mannered and conscientious.

Shrilata interrupted and said-Please! Don't tell me about the tales of the police, it's enough.

They have reached near Shankar. Both the constables were sitting near Shankar's bed. They stood up seeing the doctor. Shrikumar said-Both of you may go out for some time as I have to take out the clothes of the patient for a checkup. The constables went and stood outside the door.

After they left Shrikumar sat near Shankar and Shrilata shut the door. Shankar said slowly-Doctor, I have to leave this place tonight.

Shrikumar said-You want to go, but, how? You don't have the strength to walk properly.

Shankar said-Paresh Mahapatra may come today evening or tomorrow morning for questioning. You can't stop it for a long time, isn't it?

Shrikumar asked-How will you go?

Shankar said-You needn't worry about that. I will make the necessary arrangements. You keep the necessary medicines and prescription ready. It will be better if both of you don't stay here tonight.

Shrilata said-If we don't stay then the mother will be worried. Shrikumar said-We have plans to go out today. By the time we return it will be late at night or maybe early morning. We will tell mother the same thing. But Shankar, as a doctor my advice is- If you go away from here now, it will be dangerous for your health.

Shankar laughed and said-Is staying back less dangerous?

Shrilata said-Then let me prepare some food for you quickly.

Shrikumar said-We will also eat something and leave. Is there any certainty that we will get food at night?

Shrilata brought chappatis, curry, and milk for Shankar. She sat down near him and made him eat. After that, both of them left for home.

After having their lunch at home, they got ready to go to the distant village. In between Sundar Das had sent someone. Three of them rode the bicycles and left. A few days back Shrikumar had bought a ladies bicycle for Shrilata for her convenience.

Though it was afternoon, still it wasn't so hot in the forest. In that light and shadow, they travelled. Till now there was as such no aim and objective in Shrilata's life. The glamorous artist was now attracted towards social issues. She was stimulated and slowly advanced with the Naxalite activities without thinking deeply. There was a lot of excitement in that work-but there was no certainty in achieving a successful goal. After coming to Koraput and being in the company of Shrikumar she introspected herself.

After successfully treating a critical patient, after performing an operation successfully to save a life, the way Shrikumar is ecstatic, that was a new experience for Shrilata. These small achievements, momentary success makes life complete. That doesn't wait for anyone's acknowledgment, it is self- sufficient. Shrilata has never experienced this type of happiness in life. The Sun burns itself to give light and heat to others, the whole world survives with that. The Moon also gets it light from the reflection of the Sun. She has never experienced the joy to blaze and give light to others.

While introspecting herself, she thought about Shrikumar and was thrilled. Shrikumar was engrossed in his thoughts and was riding his bicycle. Shrilata kept her hand on his hand and said- Shrikumar if I wouldn't have met you, I wouldn't have known my inner self. Shrikumar looked at her surprisingly. He said-What happened, Shrilata , you are praising me suddenly.

Shrilata said-No, no I am not praising you. Those who didn't get an opportunity to know you properly, they can't understand, how you are self- sufficient. Shrikumar said-I am still waiting for the entirety.

Shrilata blushed-she couldn't look at Shrikumar's face. The volunteer who was with them said-Sir, We have reached near the village. We have to keep our bicycles here and have to walk.

There was a small pigeon pea field in the midst of that were seven to eight Kachha houses. That was the village. People have come from a distance of seven to eight miles to meet the doctor. Someone had come with a small child, and some had come who has been suffering from fever for a long time. There were few patients with wounds. Shrikumar examined them with lots of care, asked them about their health issues very patiently. Malaria is the major disease in the forest- other than that, dysentery and other infections. That's why he carries along with him the necessary medicines. By the time he finished the treatment and other necessary things, it was almost evening. In the forest, it gets dark by 4 pm to 5 pm. The volunteer who went along with him lit the two lanterns which he was carrying.

After that, the health education program started with 25-30 tribal people. Each center has a blackboard. Shrikumar drew the diagram on the blackboard and tried to explain them in a very simple way-How does the disease spread? What can be done to control the spread of the disease? Shrilata saw that the listeners were only nodding their heads but whether they are able to understand or not, she wasn't sure about that. She asked a tribal lady-Are you able to understand? She said- If you boil water and drink it after it cools down you won't get a disease. The lady laughed and said-What will the doctor do then? He won't come along with you. Shrilata is devoid of this hearty laugh of the tribals.

Shrikumar heard this amazing answer and said-Shrilata, did you understand, what the lady said? If you want the company of the doctor then don't give them advice regarding how not to get the disease.

Shrilata tried to be annoyed with him but laughed and said-Whether I want the company of the doctor or not, that I will decide, but why didn't she listen to my advice? Shrikumar said-A lady is sensitive towards the feelings of another lady-that's why.

After the discussion, both of them went and sat on a place in the field which was clean. The volunteer hadn't yet finished his work-he was noting down their names and address.

It was almost 8pm in the evening-but it seemed as if it's midnight in the forest. From a distance, the sound of jackals howling could be heard. The moon was rising from the other side of the mountain.

Shrikumar said-Shrilata you have stayed in the forest and mountain for a long time. I feel there is a lot of attraction in the forest-Can we ever be simple and fresh like the rabbits, deer's, and the tribals of the mountain?

Shrilata said-If we, then we would have been the victims. Today those who are hunting the rabbits and the deers, they are also making their brothers, the tribals their victim. They are so much intoxicated and obsessed with it that these simple tribal people living in the forest can't escape from the clutches of these money lenders.

Shrikumar said-That's a common thing. Is there any way out for this?

The volunteer came back. Shrilata took out tea for three of them from the thermo flask and also gave them some biscuits. Shrikumar asked-Shall we stay here at night or shall we go back?

Govinda, the volunteer said-Sir, there is no facility of staying back here. How will we sleep? Other than that there are lots of mosquitoes here, and as such, there is no problem on the way. We will hang the lanterns and ride the bicycles. By the time we reach the hospital, it will be almost 12 am. There are no wild animals on the way. Shrikumar asked-Shall we leave? Shrilata said-Yes.

They all rode on their bicycle on their way back home. Shrikumar was surprised-He thought that Shrilata is a girl from Calcutta-how can she work so hard endlessly? Other than that the forest road isn't smooth-there are so many ups and downs. It can be said that it's undulated. It's not easy to ride on a bicycle and travel on these roads. For the past few days, Shrilata has been riding on her bicycle for almost 10 to 12 miles every day regarding her work.

After covering a distance of 4 to 5 miles, there was a small spring and a rocky platform near it. The water was sparkling with the rays of the moon. Shrikumar said-Let's sit here for some time. Govinda said-Sir, the wild animals come here to drink water, we will sit here for less time and then leave.

Shrikumar and Shrilata washed their face in the spring water. They felt fresh. There was a lot of sweating because of the cycling. Shrilata was drenched in sweat and her blouse was stuck to her body. Her hair was tangled. Shrikumar looked at her enraptured. Shrilata saw this and turned her face. Shrilata's body was electrified. She had so many male friends with whom she had acted and played, but she never had this type of feelings. She quivered. She covered her face with her palms and tried to gain control over her feelings. Shrikumar noticed the changes in her. He kept his hand softly on her back and said-What happened Shrilata? Shrilata felt like leaning over Shrikumar and embracing him, but she controlled herself.

They returned back to the hospital taking the known path. They were very hungry and tired. Both of them had their food and were about to go to sleep. Suddenly Shrikumar remembered about Shankar. He said Shrilata-Let's go and meet Shankar. Shrilata didn't say anything and nodded her head as a sign of approval. Both of them went to the hospital.

Near the door, a constable was sleeping with his gun kept next to him. Shankar's bed was empty-the window near the bed was open. Both of them returned back silently. The constable was comfortably sleeping and snoring.

Chapter-18

Before the sunrise, Srilata came to wake up Shrikumar. Shrikumar was tired so he slept. After knocking at the door for 2 to 3 times, he came and opened the door. It must be around 4.30 am. Shrikumar's mother also woke up and came when she heard Shrilata knocking at Shrikumar's door. Shrilata said-The police have arrived.

Shrikumar washed his face and went to the living room. He saw DSP Vaktavastalam, Mr.Paresh Mahapatra, and the local police officer. Shrikumar told his mother to prepare tea and send it.

Vaktavastalam said-Do you know doctor, that Shankar has left the hospital?

Shrikumar said-Went? Where? He wasn't in a condition to go away.

Mr. Paresh said-I doubted that and have posted two constables to keep an eye on him, but he managed to escape.

Shrilata came with the tea. Mr. Paresh said-Yesterday night one more serious incident has happened. The rice godown of T.K Subudhi of Tenuli Gummar was ransacked. The Naxalites tied Subudhi and his sons on a pole opened the godown and distributed the rice among the tribal people.

Vaktavastalam said-Before starting their activities at any place, they do such things to attract the attention of the local people. Subudhi's accountant came stealthily and informed us, we reached there and they fired the bullets and hid in the darkness. I think the reason behind taking Shankar out of the hospital is- they might have the apprehension that we may question Mr. Shankar regarding his comrades working in Koraput and it would be better if he leaves this place before being interrogated.

Vaktavastalam paused for a while and said- After six months the Naxalites have started their activities again. T.K Subudhi brought the rice in black and sold it for a high price- I got this information. But this isn't related to our task force –otherwise, I would have raided his godown. Other than that it's the work of Odisha police-I am not at all worried for his loss; I have only apprehension-what will happen next?

Mr. Paresh said-There is one more thing doctor. In that place, there was a lady who was hurt and lying unconscious near Subudhi's house. We brought her in our jeep. With a little bit of hesitation, he said- If I am not wrong, she is pregnant.

Shrilata was listening to their discussion though she was inside the house. She came out and asked-Where is she now?

Mr.Paresh said-There is nothing to worry-I brought the nurse of the hospital from her quarter and had left the lady under her supervision. We don't know anything exactly about the woman-we only know that her name is Sushree Das.

Shrilata immediately left for the hospital. Shrikumar also took his stethoscope and left. All of them went to the hospital.

On the table of the examination room was laying a young lady-her eyes were closed. The lower part of her clothes was drenched with blood; but, there was no sign of pain on her face. She had dark, thick long hair, and sharp features. Her looks justified her name. The nurse had kept water on the stove for boiling and was wiping the blood of the patient with the cotton right from her thighs till downwards.

Shrikumar went and checked the pulse of the patient. Then he checked her heartbeat with the stethoscope and eyes with a small pencil torch. He took out the medicine from his bag, put a few drops in water, and tried to open her mouth to make her drink. He put the medicine in her mouth and again checked her pulse. Shrilata was scared and was standing behind him. She said- Mr. Paresh's doubt mayn't be wrong, but it can't be said immediately why was there an internal hemorrhage? Shrilata, kindly help the nurse and open her clothes and make it a little loose. If you can change her blood- stained clothes, it will be better. Nothing else to do now, if again the hemorrhage occurs, we will see.

Shrikumar came to his office room along with Vaktavastalam and others. Vaktavastalam said-Doctor you told me that along with Chinmaya Chakravarty there were three women. Is she one of them or somebody else?

Shrikumar said-I can't say correctly. But, how did you know that her name is Sushree Das?

Mr. Paresh said-There was a handkerchief that was tugged to her waist and on the handkerchief, it was written in Bengali-Sushree Das. That's why I think she is Sushree.

Vaktavastalam said-Till now you didn't get married doctor. You don't know that a woman never uses another woman's handkerchief.

Shrikumar said-I am inexperienced in that aspect, but I can ask Shrilata. Vaktavastalam suddenly said- What is Ms. Shrilata's work here, doctor?

Shrikumar said worriedly-She had come here for her Sociology research work. Now she is a major associate of Sundar Das and is a leader of Girijana Mahila Mandal.

Mr. Paresh said-Some of them think that you have a close relationship with her and there is a chance that you may get married to her. Shrikumar laughed- Is it so? Mr. Paresh, if you can give this good news to Ms.Shrilata I will be grateful to you. Of course, I don't have the capability to pay you the mediator fees.

Shrilata came outside the hospital and said- For my marriage, there is no requirement of a mediator. Doctor, if you are through with the discussion regarding your marriage, would you kindly go and see the patient?

Shrikumar followed Shrilata like a culprit and went to see the patient. Shrilata had already changed her clothes and the patient was lying with her eyes closed. In between, she screamed Uh! and made a little movement.

Shrikumar said- Shrilata , please get some warm milk. Shrilata brought some warm milk and gave it in her mouth with a spoon. The patient opened her eyes and looked around. Shrilata had bowed down on her face. Her eyes were fixed on Shrilata. She said-Lata! Shrilata told her-Drink the milk and sleep. You will feel better. The patient closed her eyes.

In the meantime, Mr. Paresh and Mr. Vaktavastalam came there. They said- We are leaving, doctor. Is there anything to worry about?

Shrikumar said-Nothing can be said now. The police jeep left.

Shrikumar called the nurse and said- Sit down here for some time. I will finish my daily chores and come back. He told Shrilata - It's not necessary to wait here. I will write down a prescription to give glucose saline.

Both of them went back home. Shrikumar said-She was there with you in Govindpur.

Shrilata said-Yes, her name is Sushree Das. Do you remember Chinmaya Dada had told you there that the name of these three ladies begins with 'S'-Actually our name is like that-Her name is Sushree and the other one's name is Sodashi. He always said that according to the beginning alphabet of our name.

Shrikumar asked-Where is her house?

Shrilata said- She belongs to East Bengal-during the partition they came and stayed in Calcutta .Nageswar Rao had rented a house near Ms. Sushree's house. At that time she was studying at Calcutta University. Sushree has a melodious voice. She sometimes goes and participates in the program. She was a student at that time. She is very good at Hindustani and Carnatic style of music. At that time she was learning it. One day after the program, when she was returning home 3 to 4 gong of the society stopped her. The people in the society closed their doors as they saw these ferocious gongs.

The rickshaw puller left the rickshaw and fled. Ms. Sushree pleaded to them, but they didn't leave her. They tore her clothes and made her almost naked. Refugee family-Why will anyone help them? At that time Nageswar Rao was returning home on his bicycle. Sushree in helplessness lay down in front of his bicycle-She said-Dada, please save me. Nageswar Rao stopped. He tried to make the gongs understand, threatened them that he will hand over them to the police. But, demons don't have sympathy. Finally, he had to face the three alone. He was wounded. He took Sushree and left her in her house.

But, the misfortune didn't end there. The gongs were ready to take revenge. One day they came and threatened

Sushree's family-They told them to leave her along with them, otherwise, there will be bloodshed. Sushree's family was her blind mother, drug addicted brother, and sister in law. Her family pushed Sushree towards them and closed the door. At that time, a small boy of the society went and informed Nageswar Rao. He fought with all of them with a stick. It wasn't possible for them to stay in Calcutta-that night they sat in a truck and went to Vijaywada.

Shrikumar took a deep breath and said-Life is strange!

Shrilata said- They went to Vijayawada, Vijayanagram, Madras, and many more places. Sometimes Ms. Sushree sings and also she is a very good Veena player other than that she can read, write and speak Hindi, Odia, and Bengali.

Shrikumar asked-Did she marry Nageswar Rao?

Shrilata said-No, she didn't. But both of them understand each other very well. If one of them gives the indication, the other one can understand. Ms.Sushree- is a lady with independent thoughts, but she trusts Nageswar Rao a lot.Ms. Sushree accepts whatever he says without questioning.

Shrikumar asked-Was she there during the raid? Shrilata said-I can't say.Chinmaya Da doesn't involve the ladies in action programs. The main thing is –we aren't very perfect at shooting. Of course, among the three of us, she is more perfect.

There was a lot of apprehension, confusion, and reluctance in Shrikumar's mind when he heard this. He knows-When required, the rebels shoot. He felt restless when he thought that his good friends, Prasanta, Shankar, and Shrilata's hands are smeared with human blood. He asked in a feeble voice-Shrilata, did you ever shoot anyone?

Shrilata said-No, I didn't face any such situation. But,

if it would have been required I would have shot. She laughed and said-Maybe it's not required anymore. She looked at Shrikumar affectionately and said-Shrikumar, you have changed my perspective. Shrikumar gaped at her.

In the afternoon Shrilata went and sat near Ms. Sushree. She cooked for her and took it. Around 4 pm Shrikumar finished his work in the hospital and came near Sushree's bed. He checked her blood pressure and pulse and said-There is nothing to worry. Ms.Sushree, how are you feeling now?

Sushree said- I am feeling a little weak. Can I get up and walk around?

Shrikumar said-No, you have to take a rest for at least 24 hrs. Though there is nothing much to worry about, but I am not able to find out what caused the haemorrhage. Did you fall anywhere?

At that time Mr.Paresh and Vaktavastalam arrived. They sat on the chairs on one side of the patient and on the other side Shrikumar and Shrilata sat.

Mr.Paresh asked-How is she now? Can I ask her a few questions now?

Before the doctor could say anything Ms. Sushree said-You may ask.

Mr. Paresh asked- When did you go to Subudhi's house? How many of them were there in your group? Who gave you the information about Subudhi's rice godown?

Ms.Sushree said-I think, you think that I was in the gang which ransacked.

Mr.Paresh said-I think so.

Ms.Sushree said- I am teaching music to the girls in Subudhi's house for past three months. They have given me a house near their rice godown. I go there twice a week, and whenever I come, I stay in that house at night. Mr. Paresh asked-Who else stay with you in that house?

Ms. Sushree said-Who else will stay? At night his servant comes and sleeps in the living room. He sweeps the house and provides drinking water.

Mr.Paresh said-Tell us, what happened last night.

Sushree said-It was almost 2 am.I was sleeping. The boy sleeping in the living room screamed and woke me up. He said-Didi, get up, there are dacoits. I didn't believe him at first-but, I woke up and saw that there were many people outside. I didn't go near them-I saw that from the godown the rice bags were carried outside and someone was distributing it among the people. I gathered my courage and went near. Someone told me-You go back to the house-no one will harm you. After 10 to 15 minutes I heard the sound of the jeep and then what happened, I don't know.

Mr. Paresh asked- Where is your house? Sushree said-I belong to a refugee family in East Bengal. I learned music and studied in my childhood. I teach music to children in different places and earn my living. At present, I am staying in a rented house with a few more girls in Koraput town.

Mr. Paresh asked- What about your parents and your other family members?

Sushree said-They were staying in Calcutta. I don't know where they are now. I left them almost 7 years back. I don't have any relationship with them. Then she told the doctor-I want to drink some water, I am feeling weak. Shrilata handed over the glass filled with water to her. Shrikumar said- Mr. Paresh,You may stop questioning now. It's not good to pressurize her in this condition.

Mr.Vaktavastalam said-I will ask only one question. He said- You travelled from Koraput to here to take music tuitions. Who introduced you to Subudhi's family?

Ms. Sushree smiled and said-Who will introduce me? I go to the Music College in Koraput during their function. Subudhi's elder son stays in Koraput regarding business matters. He told me to come to Tentulimunda and take the tuitions.

Mr.Paresh and Mr.Vaktavastalam stood up. Mr. Paresh asked- How is her health now? How many more days is she going to stay in the hospital?

Shrikumar said-At least for a week.

Mr. Paresh smiled and said-We may leave now. But, she shouldn't escape like Mr. Shankar.

Shrikumar said firmly-My duty is to treat the patient, nothing more or less than that.

Mr. Paresh and Mr. Vaktavastalam left. After they left Shrikumar asked-Whatever you told them, is that true?

Ms. Sushree said-Of course. Outwardly it's true. Subudhi's family can't deny that I was taking tuitions. But, what was my intention behind that is a different matter-it's not necessary for me to tell the police regarding it. Shrikumar said-I didn't believe that the police will accept your statement and leave. I thought they will ask you many questions.

Sushree said-To stop that, the doctor is there. If there are any apprehensions about the patient's life a doctor can stop the police from interrogating –Don't you know that? Shrikumar said-We can think about it later on. Get well soon.

Sushree said- A friend like Shrilata, can bring you back from the doors of death by her nursing skills. There is no chance to lay in bed sick.

The next day Shrikumar went to visit Sushree. Ms. Sushree was leaning on a pillow and was sitting. Shrilata was sitting next to her and was talking.

Ms. Sushree looked at Shrikumar and said-I will ask you a question. I hope that, you will tell me the truth.

Shrikumar said-You may ask.

Ms.Sushree asked-How is the baby in my womb? Will he survive?

Shrikumar wasn't ready for this question. He tried to hide his uneasiness and took out the stethoscope immediately. He asked-When did you conceive?

Sushree said-More than 4 months. Almost 5 months.

Shrikumar asked- Can you feel the movement of the child?

Ms.Sushree said- Yes, sometimes I feel that.

Shrikumar checked her tummy with a stethoscope. He could hear a faint sound and a slow movement. He said-The baby is safe. To know in detail about the baby, you need to undergo a few tests. We don't have that facility here. Convey my best wishes to the baby's father.

Ms. Sushree said- To the father-Why to the father? You should wish me. I wanted a baby.

Shrikumar said-That's right, but according to the social norms, your husband—

Ms. Sushree said -Husband? I didn't get married.

Shrikumar looked at her face dumbfounded.

Ms. Sushree looked at his face intently for some time and said- Doctor, you have read life sciences. You know that the baby grows in the mother's womb for 280 days right from the day it is conceived till birth-the baby grows and becomes healthy by sucking the mother's blood. According to the scientific viewpoint, the necessity of the father isn't more than 5 to 7 minutes. Still for the birth of the baby, you will convey your good wishes to the father-Is it justified according to the sciences?

Shrikumar never thought in this way-All his thoughts

were muddled up. He said-But according to the social norms—

Ms. Sushree said- In India there are many mother centered societies. She raised her eyebrows and said-What has this society given me, for which I will leave the scientific aspect and adhere to the social norms, rules, and regulations?

Shrikumar couldn't say anything-He looked at her face like a fool.

Ms. Sushree said-Is it not much wiser to understand the truth rather than following the old history?

Shrikumar understood that Ms. Sushree is educated; according to her there is enough justification for her argument. Still, he couldn't accept it as he was an old-fashioned schoolboy.

Shrilata said-Sushree Di, you don't try to make him understand much. The doctor has become insane with this shock treatment. For him, life means- sober and serene-getting married to a lady with garland, band party, priest, and friends. After that children—

Sushree said-No Lata. I won't do so much injustice to the doctor. He is a simple and ingenuous person. I have gone through lots of troubles and life has tested me time and again but, he is free from all these. Let him remain ethereal and ingenuous. You are lucky, you have got his company.

Shrikumar looked at Shrilata's face.

Shrilata was blushing. Her face looked bright and cheerful. To change the topic she said-I can't imagine-Shree Di-if the police wouldn't have brought you, what would have happened.

Sushree said in an unacquisitive voice- What would have happened! At this stage whatever happens to a lady working in the mines, in a tea garden, in the fields, or as a laborer, the same thing would have happened with me. That's why Mr. Rao told me several times, in these revolutionary activities, I shouldn't be inclined towards this type of thoughts. She smiled and said-Lata, since the day I met him, this is for the first time that I didn't listen to his advice.

Shrikumar said-According to psychology, for a woman, to become a mother is the most sought and the most intense desire.

Sushree said-Maybe. But for me, there is another need. Staying alone for months together-in the sleepless night sometimes I feel that social philosophy, revolution, music are all meaningless. To evade this lonliness, if there would have been a child? By playing with him, being engaged with him time would have passed smoothly. You mayn't be able to understand it doctor, how painful is the loneliness.

Shrilata mocked at the doctor and said- The doctor isn't lonely, he won't be able to understand it. One of my uncles is a doctor-my aunt always complains-she says-Lata, you never get married to a doctor. Life will become barren. The doctor will be busy with his patients and you have to keep waiting for him.

Sushree laughed. Shrikumar showed unreal sadness on his face and said- Shrilata,I work in the forest region of Koraput ,I don't do private practice nor have landed property or vehicle to attract any woman. Today after listening to Mr. Paresh, a ray of hope aroused in me. I thought I have reached my destination. But I never knew that you have so much aversion for doctors. I have to tell this to my police friends. They are very active-they can suggest an alternative way. Ms. Sushree again laughed.

Shrikumar and Shrilata left for the house. On the way, Shrilata stopped Shrikumar, held his hand, looked at his face, and asked- You have become very vocal now a days. Previously, you were too silent and when questioned, you never replied. You were always grave. Is it because of the touch of Ms.Sushree?

Shrikumar said- The touch of anyone can't create a ripple within me. Don't you know, your touch has changed me from a silent person to a talkative one?

Shrilata kept her hands on his lips and said-It's ok, if you say everything beforehand then like Ms. Sushree you have to spend many sleepless nights. Both of them returned home.

Chapter-19

After three weeks the chief of the labourers recovered. He was taken from the hospital and kept in the police lock- up. Because of Sundar Das's effort a case was filed against him. He was trying his best to get a bail but the magistrate didn't grant him bail. He was sent to Koraput jail.

In the meantime Sushree had recovered but Shrilata was reluctant to leave her. Sometimes all of them together went to visit the nearby mountain. Shrikumar's mother also understood the health condition of Sushree and took a lot of care of her.

One evening a jeep came and stopped near Shrikumar's house. Mr. Vaktavastalam and Mrs. Meera Vaktavastalam got down from the jeep. Mr. Vaktavastalam was in a white trouser and a silk kurta-Mrs.Vaktavastalam was in a designer Kanjivaram silk saree. Both of them came with a smiling face and wished. Mrs. Meera said Shrikumar- You have forgotten us. You didn't visit us again.

Shrikumar brought them into the house. What a surprise! It's beyond my imagination. Please! Sit down. Then he went inside the house where Shrilata and Sushree were sitting. Shrikumar knew Shrilata's attitude towards the police- he called her alone and said-Mrs.

Vaktavastalam had come. She had treated me well as a guest. Please, don't show your anger in front of her.

Shrilata said-What! Do you think, I don't know how to behave in front of the guests? You may go and give them the company. We will come.

Shrikumar went to the living room. Mrs. Meera said-I heard that there is a musician in your house. I have a lot of interest in music- but never got an opportunity to practice. Mr. Vaktavastalam said- I told her, it will be an interruption to the doctor's privacy. But she insisted on-Please! Don't blame me.

Srilata and Sushree came to the room. Mrs. Meera wished them. Both of them had dressed up simply but they were looking beautiful. Before Shrikumar could say anything,Mr .Vaktavastalam gave the introduction of both of them and said-She is Ms. Banerjee, a researcher in Sociology, and the leader of Koraput's Girijan Mahila Samiti and she is Ms. Sushree. I have already told you about them. Then she pointed at Mrs. Meera and said-She is my wife. Till now the conversation was going on in English. Mrs. Meera asked surprisingly- How can you speak Telugu so fluently?

Sushree said-For a few days I was in Vijayawada.

Mr. Vaktavastalam asked- Where did you stay in Vijayawada? Mrs. Meera stopped him abruptly and said-We have come here to listen to her music-not for your investigation. Who stayed in Vijayawada or Bombay-What will we get out of that? You are cultured and a music lover-in the future, at least till you are with me, you have to overcome your curiosity. Then she said Sushree- You have to sing and play Veena for me. I have come here with lots of expectations.

Sushree said-I sing classical music. At present due

to my health issues, I can't sing. I could have played the Veena, but there is no Veena here.

Mrs.Meera said-I apprehended that. You were there in the hospital for treatment, so from where will you bring the Veena; that's why I have brought the Veena. She instructed the driver to bring the instrument from the jeep. She had also brought a Tablachi along with her.

Ms. Sushree inspected the Veena and then started playing it. She played Ahir Bhairav Raag and the music filled the house. She closed her eyes slowly. In Shrikumar's house in that silent forest, the music was echoing. Mrs .Meera sat there captivated by the music. Shrikumar, Shrilata and Mr.Vaktavastalam were dumbstruck. After 50 minutes when Sushree stopped playing the raga, Mr. Vaktavastalam said- I have never heard such soul- touching music. Ms. Sushree, you have magic in your hands.

Shrilata said-Listen to her voice some other day, you will be surprised. In Calcutta, many singers and musicians use to come to our house, but they aren't comparable with Sushree Di. Her song and music are heavenly. Mrs. Meera, Please! Sing a song for us.

Mrs. Meera sang a Telugu devotional song as all of them requested her. Mrs. Meera's voice was sweet, but she lacked practice. Mr. Vaktavastalam said-You may come once to Ichapur and stay in our house for a few days. Sushree said-I don't have plans to go outside now. I will let you know afterward. Mrs. Meera said-Let's leave now. You may keep the Veena. My uncle stays in Koraput, we will stay there tonight. Both of them left in their jeep.

After listening to the music Shrikumar was sitting spellbound. He was thinking-In this country many talented people lose their identity as they aren't recognized. Sushree may be caught by the police regarding some revolutionary activities and will be sentenced to death or imprisoned.

Shrikumar slowly said- We should be obliged to Mrs. Meera .If she wouldn't have brought the Veena today we wouldn't have experienced this heavenly music. At that time Nageswar Rao came from behind. He said-I am thankful from my side, doctor. I haven't heard Shree playing Veena for a long time. I am contented now. Sushree saw him and got up. She asked-How did you come? Nageswar Rao said- A dead person also becomes alive after listening to your music,Shree. Sushree said-Please! Sit down; I will play for you lifelong. Nageswar Rao said-I am ill- fated, Shree. I couldn't quench my thirst though being in the banks of the river Ganges. There was happiness in Sushree's face. She said-Did I ever say you 'No'? Sushree was holding Nageswar Rao's hand and was comforting him.

Shrilata was silent till then. She said, Dada, how did you come here suddenly?

Nageswar Rao said- I have come to see Shree. I saw the police jeep-I had a doubt, whether they have come to take her? Later on, I saw that Mr. Vaktavastalam and a lady getting down from the jeep. Then from the arrangements, I came to know that it was an arrangement made for music. I thought-I will hide and listen. I was thinking-If Shree can play Ahir Bhairav. She knows that it's my favorite raga. I am blessed-I heard the raga today. Ms. Sushree became emotional and kept her head on his lap. Nageswar Rao caressed her hair and said- What does Shree mean for me, I can't understand that doctor. Chinmaya Da says that I have a soft corner for her, but I know Shree is my real strength and power. But for me, she couldn't prosper in her career or in music.

Shrikumar had never seen this face of Nageswar Rao's personality. A strong person like him has such a soft heart, can't be perceived unless seen in person.

After a long time, Sushree raised her head. Her eyes were filled with tears. Shrilata with a lot of love and affection wiped her face with her saree. Sushree went inside the house to wash her face.

Shrilata said-Dada, don't worry, Sushree Di is fine. I won't leave her from here for at least a month.

Nageswar Rao asked-What's the activity of the police? Do they suspect Shree?

Shrikumar said-In the beginning Mr. Paresh suspected that she belonged to the invader's group. But later on, after speaking to her, maybe he doesn't suspect her. He may come once again.

Nageswar Rao said- Because of her present condition I tried to keep her away from all these. But she is very stubborn-where ever I stay, she will stay there. Finally, such an arrangement was made where no one can suspect her. I am relaxed now as you have taken her responsibility, doctor.

Ms. Sushree came out and said-I have given my responsibility to one single person. He can't shift his responsibility. Nageswar Rao laughed. His laugh was adorable. He said-This is a temporary arrangement, not permanent. I may leave now. While he was going outside the house Shrilata asked-Dada, how is Sodashi? Nageswar Rao said –She went from Govindpur camp to Midinapore. I don't have much information about her. Shrilata again asked-How is Chinmaya Da? Nageswar Rao didn't say anything. He remained silent. Shrilata understood that it's better not to ask this question.

Nageswar Rao went towards the forest. Sushree

followed him for a distance. Shrilata and Shrikumar stayed back.

Ms.Sushree returned. She remained silent for a while and said- You might have felt bad doctor, but after seeing Mr. Rao I was overwhelmed. After I saw him I felt that whatever sweetness is there within me, if I could have squeezed all that for him? A person who hasn't seen him closely can never realize his true personality. In his angry grave personality is hidden, forgiveness, and lots of love. He is ready to gulp the entire poison in this world without hesitation. He never thinks about himself. He is an extraordinary human being.

Shrikumar and Shrilata were listening to her enchanted.

After having food Shrikumar went to his room but couldn't sleep till late night. It was a moonlit night and many thoughts came to his mind.

At that time he heard the music from the Veena. May be Ms. Sushree didn't sleep and also she got a chance to play Veena after such a long time. He heard the Thumri of Bade Gulam Ali. This song sung by him had become very famous worldwide-Kaa karu Sajani,ayae na balam-It means – I waited for you - My love you didn't come-what will I do now ,my beloved - the heart touching music from the Veena filled the forest with discontent and sorrow. Time and again the music was played-Kaa karun sajani. It seemed as if the earth and the sky mourned. The fluttering sound of the leaf and chirping of the bird turned into lament.

After a long time, the music stopped. Shrikumar came back to his bed and saw Shrilata standing in the darkness. He touched her face and realized that she was crying. With lots of love, Shrikumar lifted her face and wiped her tears. Shrilata embraced him. She quivered in his arms. The music had stopped long back –but it was lingering in Shrikumar's mind and resounding in his ears - Kaa karun Sajani…

■■

BLACK EAGLE BOOKS

www.blackeaglebooks.org
info@blackeaglebooks.org

Black Eagle Books, an independent publisher, was founded as
a nonprofit organization in April, 2019. It is our mission to
connect and engage the Indian diaspora and the world at large
with the best of works of world literature published on a
collaborative platform, with special emphasis on
foregrounding Contemporary Classics and New Writing.